SHADOW OF THE SKYTREE

K. J. TAYLOR

ODYSSEY
BOOKS

Published by Odyssey Books in 2019
www.odysseybooks.com.au

 A catalogue record for this book is available from the National Library of Australia

ISBN: 978-1-925652-79-6 (paperback)
ISBN: 978-1-925652-80-2 (ebook)

Cover design by Michelle Lovi

PROLOGUE: FIRE AND SMOKE

The great volcano stood in the middle of a blasted plain, and all about there was suffocating heat and smoke. At its base the city lay, carved from the living rock, but now the streets and the houses were deserted except for the skulking, shaggy forms that squatted in doorways, feeding on the dead.

The elf standing on a balcony carved into the side of the volcano itself took all of this in, and his expression did not so much as flicker, though he felt sick to the very bottom of his soul. The smoke was in his lungs and it burned at him with every breath, the stench of decay wafting up from the city making him want to vomit.

He glanced up, seeing the sickly yellow of the sky, and more than anything he wanted to be away from this place. He needed trees and clear skies, and clean water. He had seen too much horror. Had tasted too much horror.

While he stood and brooded, someone else came up beside him.

'Lyell,' she murmured.

His stomach lurched at the sight of her face. 'Everything is finished now,' he muttered back. 'It's over.'

The dwarf woman wordlessly stared down at the ruined city and the dull light played over her face. Standing side by side, they were a match of opposites: he was tall and slender, black-haired, skin the brown of aged wood, and golden eyes; she was as short as a human, black-skinned, stocky and powerful, her hair blond, and her eyes blue and silver. Now those eyes were red-rimmed and weeping, and yet they grew a little warmer when she looked at him.

'My city is finished,' she said. 'My race is finished. You and I have been doing the best we could, but it was not enough. Perhaps, then, this is what the gods decreed. Plague, civil war, kobolds ravaging... all of it so fast. It is as if the world itself is ending.'

'I know exactly what you mean, Agafya,' Lyell said in a flat voice, thinking that he did indeed know. Somewhere deep inside himself something was screaming, but as before he ignored it. Slowly, methodically, he reached for the dagger at his side. He had done all he had been bidden to do, and now it was time to finish it.

Agafya gave him an agonised look. 'Everyone fell ill—what was it that I was being the only survivor? The only one who did not die? Over and over I have been asking myself this question, but now I think I know the answer.'

Lyell hesitated. 'What?'

'I am having something to live for, my love,' she replied softly. 'And that is you.' She clasped his hand. 'Our time together, it was the greatest joy I have ever been knowing in all my life.'

He tensed. 'Agafya—'

'Take me with you!' she said, suddenly fierce. 'This place is no home for me or anyone else. We can leave and make a new life for ourselves, together! And who would be caring that I am a dwarf and you are an elf? I love you and you love me, so let us be together!'

The dagger was in Lyell's free hand now, hidden behind his back. He gritted his teeth. A quick stab through the ribs would be all it would take, and it would be done. His orders were clear. There could be—must not be—any survivors.

And yet...

'I love you,' said Agafya. 'Say something! Lyell—'

The elf's back heaved and with a quick impulsive movement he dropped the dagger and took her in his arms. 'There is no time, and this place is not safe,' he whispered in her ear. 'We must go, *now*.'

1

LAVENDER AND FIORELLA

Fiorella was hard at work as usual, bending over a pot on the stove that gave off a steady stream of yellowish fumes. From time to time she checked the mercury temperature gauge that poked out of the potion and adjusted the flame beneath the pot by turning a brass knob.

Lavender sat up on a shelf by the desk and watched with interest. 'Is it working this time?'

Fiorella glanced up. 'I think so. I'll try another dose today.' She stopped suddenly and started to cough, fumbling for a handkerchief. Blood spattered onto the white cloth, and after a short interval the coughing wheezed to a stop.

Lavender stood up. 'How are you? Do you feel worse today, or better?'

Fiorella took a deep breath. 'About the same,' she said hoarsely. 'But this *is* the right mixture, I'm sure of it.' She quickly turned her attention back to the steaming pot. 'I just need to get the dosage right. There's something I'm doing wrong, but I'm not sure what.'

'You can do it.' Lavender hopped off the shelf and onto the

desk, which was covered in scattered papers. 'I know you can. You're the cleverest human there is.' She grinned.

Fiorella laughed weakly. 'All humans are clever,' she said. 'We have to be, to survive without magic.'

'But you don't live that long,' Lavender added.

'No, and our lives are growing even shorter now with this cursed plague,' said Fiorella. She muttered a curse word under her breath. 'If someone doesn't find a cure, and soon, we could go the way of the dwarves. But please keep quiet for a while, Lavender. I need to concentrate.'

'All right.' Lavender turned her attention to the desk where a book lay open, full of Fiorella's notes, but though she could read them they didn't mean much to her. Instead, she padded over to a second book leaning against the wall. It was as tall as her and took some effort to lift it and lay it on the floor.

It was her favourite book—the same one Fiorella had used to teach her to read human text. Lavender traced the lettering with one hand and murmured the words under her breath.

'The elves be the longest lived of all the people of this world, which they call Hylah. Their realm is the mighty forest in the north, where the great Sky Tree is the source of the River Wend. The Skytree clan rules over their people, and the Sky Tree be their home and stronghold. All elves hold power over plants, which they revere most highly. It is said that when an elf dies, he becomes a tree.'

All elves hold power over plants, which they revere most highly. Lavender grinned to herself. Now that would be a sight to remember.

'What are you doing over there?' Fiorella called.

'Practising me reading,' Lavender replied.

'*My* reading,' the human corrected.

'My reading,' said Lavender.

'That's better. Keep working at it.'

'I will.' Lavender looked around at the single room of Fiorella's home. It was a cosy place, lined with bookshelves and cupboards full of scientific equipment. A large brown owl dozed on a perch by an open window. Fiorella's bed was by the door, covered in a quilt she had made herself, though she didn't often sleep these days. She always seemed to be working. And when she *did* go to bed, Lavender would hear her coughing all night. But she'd always been like that, ever since Lavender had come here.

Lavender had a bed here, too, in the bookshelf where several books had been removed to make room for it. Her people usually slept underground, but Lavender was now used to her high-up bed, and even liked it. There was so much to see from up off the ground. And the books she'd learned to read had so much more to offer. There was a whole *world* out there, and she could see parts of it just by looking at marks on paper.

She turned another page and paused to admire the picture. It was of a pair of gnomes, a man and a woman. Like her, they had pale skin from having lived most of their lives underground, and like her they had large pointed ears and equally pointed features. But unlike her they were brightly dressed, in red hats and yellow jerkins.

'*That's* not so good an idea,' she said to herself, unconsciously slipping back into her childhood dialect. 'Dressing like that would get you kilt right quick in the forest.' She adjusted her own hat, which was a much more sensible, drab brown affair, close-fitting and sewn out of rat leather.

She turned another couple of pages and soon found her favourite one of all. A picture of a monster leaped out: big and hunched, with shaggy black fur. Its face was—what was that word Fiorella used?—bestial. Yes, that was it. Like an animal. It had a short muzzle full of dripping fangs, and long sharp claws on its hands and feet. Its eyes were red and glaring.

'Kobold,' Lavender said to herself. She was grinning again as she stroked the inked picture. She'd never seen a kobold before, but everyone knew about them and she'd read all about them in this book too. She did it again now, going over the words she'd learned so well. 'Savage beasts with neither language nor culture, they have no home but lurk at the edges of civilisation, preying upon man, elf, and dwarf alike. They are scavengers and flesh-eaters and carry the most deadly of diseases. Even to look upon a kobold can strike down the strongest.'

'So it can,' Fiorella called over her shoulder. 'And so it has. Kobolds were the source of this plague, and the plague that destroyed the dwarves.'

'Do you think the elves will catch a plague too?' asked Lavender.

'One day, perhaps. They've been lucky so far. Why don't you make yourself useful and see off those rats under the floorboards? I heard them scratching around again last night.'

'Oh, they just want to live,' said Lavender, but she closed the book and pushed it aside. An adventure under the floorboards sounded like fun.

'Maybe they do, but not at my expense they won't,' said Fiorella. 'And this time chase them off properly, will you?'

'Sure, sure.' Lavender jumped off the edge of the desk. It was quite a long way down, but she landed neatly on her feet and scampered off toward the owl's perch. The owl stirred and peered down at her. Lavender held out her arms and swayed from side to side. *'Morning now, not for hunt,'* she said, speaking the fast, clicking, hissing language of owls.

The owl clicked his beak. '*Sleep now,*' he answered, and tucked his head under his wing.

Lavender left him in peace and crouched to stick her hands into a hole in the floorboard beneath his perch. The board lifted away, and she pushed it aside with some effort and hopped down into the hole beneath.

Her large eyes adjusted to the darkness in seconds, and she immediately felt herself relax. All gnomes felt safest underground. It was their natural place to be, after all.

Through the dust and gloom, she could see the house's brick foundations, a spare gas bottle for the stove, and not much else other than a heap of assorted garbage not far away, which definitely shouldn't have been there. Lavender sniffed the air and caught the musty whiff of rat. They must have come back to their nest.

She drew her long rabbit bone knife and made for the nest.

Its owners had already smelled her. Before she had gone very far, a big female rat emerged. She was about half Lavender's size, her fur brown and oily eyes gleaming in the faint light shining between the floorboards. The animal's long teeth were already bared.

'*You, you go!*' she chattered.

Lavender raised the knife. '*You go!*' she retorted. '*Not home. Owl!*'

The rat did not back down, even at the threat of the owl. '*Home, home nest,*' she insisted. '*You go!*' She was already bristling, turning sideways and arching her back to make herself look bigger.

Lavender paused and sniffed again. Rats weren't usually this hostile. Unless...

'*Pups?*' she suggested.

'*Litter nest*,' the rat answered. She was tensing now, eyes bulging. '*Fight, fight for pup!*'

Now Lavender understood. She put her knife away and bowed. '*No fight*,' she promised. '*Friend.*'

The mother rat started to relax, but said '*Fight pup*' again, just in case.

'*No fight*,' Lavender said. She reached out a hand. '*Friend.*'

As usual, her gift worked. The rat's fur flattened and she sniffed at Lavender's hand. Her eyes were bright with intelligence, and her moist pink nose twitched rapidly.

Lavender stroked her head between the ears, scratching the spot. The rat chuckled appreciatively and then turned away, heading back to her nest. Lavender followed, knowing there was no danger now.

The nest had been carefully made: bits of scrap paper, leaves, even shed owl feathers, all bundled up to make a comfortable little cave. Lavender squeezed in after the rat, which went straight back to the hollow where her pups were huddled together. They were only a few days old, each one about as long as Lavender's forearm. Their eyes were sealed shut, ears flat against their heads, and they had no fur yet. They whiffled and squeaked as their mother groomed them, their toothless mouths already fumbling for her teats.

'*Pups, pups*,' the mother crooned. '*Feed, feed now. Safe.*'

Lavender petted one of them, feeling the soft warm skin. The pup squeaked at her and tried to suckle at her fingers. '*Friend*,' Lavender told it. '*Gnome friend.*'

The mother was watching her, but with no concern or aggression. '*Gnome friend*,' she agreed.

'*You stay*,' said Lavender. '*Stay, home.*'

She gently guided the protesting pup over to its mother and siblings and left them there in peace. On the way back, she wondered if she should lie to Fiorella. It wouldn't be fair to do that. The truth was better. Fiorella wouldn't be happy about it, but Lavender had already learned that the human didn't understand some things, no matter how clever she was about everything else.

When she climbed back up through the hole, she saw right away that Fiorella wasn't going to ask her anything right now. She was at the stove, spitting human swear words, her whole head engulfed in a cloud of yellow steam. The medicine was boiling over, hissing as it evaporated on the stove. Fiorella tried to take the pot off the heat, but she fumbled with the handle and the whole lot crashed onto the floor, spilling the last dregs onto the rug.

'Yikes!' Lavender kicked the loose floorboard aside and ran forward. 'What a mess!'

Fiorella was coughing again, and crying. 'No, no, no!'

Lavender skirted around the steaming puddle on the floor. The fumes got into her nose and made her sneeze. 'Deep spirits, it's all gone!'

Fiorella slumped onto the bed, head in her hands, and sobbed her frustration. 'I was so *close...*'

Lavender climbed up the quilt and hopped up onto the bedpost. 'What happened?'

Fiorella took a shaky breath and dabbed at her eyes. 'Oh, the fumes made me dizzy and I stopped concentrating... I barely have enough ingredients left as it is, and now I'll have to start all over again.'

Lavender frowned. 'Can I find them for you? The ingredients?'

The human looked up, red-eyed. 'Well...'

''Cause I could find them, I could,' said Lavender. 'If they're in the forest, I'll find 'em so I will.'

'Well,' Fiorella dabbed at her eyes, 'if you can find me some split leaf sage—'

'I will!' Lavender said at once. 'How much?'

'As much as you can carry, and be careful it doesn't have any scale bugs on it.'

'I'll go right now,' Lavender promised. She jumped down off the bedpost and gave Fiorella a reassuring pat on the leg. 'It's all going to be fine. You're going to do it, you are. You're too smart to not do it.'

Fiorella smiled down at her. 'Thank you, Lavender. You don't know how much help you've been to me all this time.'

'Well, well, without you I wouldn't know anything at all,' said Lavender. 'That's good payment.'

'I would say so,' said Fiorella.

Lavender grinned at her and slid off the bed and onto the floor. There was a door her size set into the human-sized one, and she went through it and out into the sunshine. She knew exactly who could help her now.

Fiorella's cottage was a long way from any other human's house, close to the River Wend. She had come here from the city after she caught the plague, to search for a cure far away from other humans who might catch the disease from her. Lavender had found her out in the garden one day—the same garden she walked through now. It was full of herbs, but fruit and nut trees and vegetables also grew there. A goat was teth-ered outside the fence, busy grazing. It bleated a hello to Lavender as she ducked under the lowest rung and headed into the meadow.

It was a sunny day, though the light hurt Lavender's eyes

and the sun would burn her skin if she stayed out in it too long. She sniffed at a flower and pushed through a tuft of grass, busy searching. They had to be here somewhere.

Sure enough, before she'd gone too far, the grass rustled and something big loomed into view. Its fur was soft brown, and a bright green grass stem hung from its mouth. The animal nibbled rapidly, big dark eyes fixed on her.

'*Morning, morning,*' Lavender greeted it. '*Friend gnome?*'

The hare's ears rose. '*Friend gnome,*' he agreed.

Lavender stroked his twitching nose. '*We run? Run now?*'

The hare paused to scratch his flank. '*Run now,*' he said after a moment.

Lavender climbed onto his back and gripped his fur. '*Run! Run, forest!*'

The hare bolted.

Lavender held on tightly and whooped with excitement. She had ridden on hare-back before, but it never lost its thrill. The sheer speed, the way the animal's long legs ate up the ground, never seeming to miss a stroke, the wind on her face... it was pure joy. She let go with one hand and pulled her hat down, though her hair had already escaped from it and whipped over her neck and shoulders. It would get tangled, but that was all part of the fun.

The hare knew which way to go. He left the meadow behind and made for the trees beyond. They were bluebark trees, their trunks slate grey and their long leaves pale green. Autumn had left a dry brown carpet underpaw, but the litter scarcely made a sound.

The hare slowed now but pressed on deeper into the forest where the undergrowth was thicker. Lavender knew the place very well and she kept her eyes open, watching for any sign of the herb Fiorella wanted. It had to be here somewhere. It wasn't rare.

Sure enough, she soon saw what they were after. She called to the hare to stop, and he sat on his haunches, making her slide down off his back. He stayed there and browsed on some yellowspot leaves, while Lavender inspected the sage.

It was the right kind, each greyish leaf neatly forked, and when she turned them over she found no trace of scale bugs or fungus. Satisfied, she drew her knife and started to cut.

Just as the first branch came away in her hand, a voice from inside the plant shouted. 'Hey!'

Lavender fell back, holding the herb. 'Who's there?' she shouted back, startled.

The leaves rustled and the speaker emerged. It was another gnome, dressed in green. His eyes were green as well. 'Lavender!' he said. 'Is it you for true?'

She relaxed. 'Bramble. Yes, it's me for you.'

Bramble prodded her in the chest. 'We thought you was dead for sure, we did.'

'I'm not,' said Lavender. 'Why'd you think that?'

'Well, our father said you was dead to him, he did,' said Bramble. 'Leaving us like that, to live with a human!'

Lavender scowled. 'Nothing wrong with that! Fiorella taught me to read, you know, and plenty of other things too.'

'Hah,' said Bramble. 'You speak like a human, you do. What of the tribe?'

'The tribe doesn't need me,' said Lavender. 'Our father has enough daughters. Anyway, I have other things I want to do.'

Bramble put his head on one side. 'What other things?'

'After Fiorella finds the cure, we'll go to the human city together,' said Lavender. 'And maybe I'll live there, or go to other places.'

He only seemed puzzled by that. '*What* other places?'

'There are places other than Bluedell,' said Lavender. 'Hundreds of them. Places you can't even imagine, but I've seen them in Fiorella's books.'

'But why would you *want* to?'

That caught her off-guard. 'Because I do, that's all,' she said lamely. 'Now I have to pick these herbs for Fiorella. Will you help me?'

Bramble drew his own knife and started to cut the sage stems. 'You talk of such strange things,' he grumbled. 'You were always different, but now you are even different-er.'

'That's not a word,' Lavender said helpfully.

'What isn't?'

'Different-er. It's not a word.'

Bramble shook his head. 'You make me no sense, Lavender.'

'If so, then so,' she answered in the old way. 'There, that should be enough.'

She and Bramble bundled the sage together, and he gave her a quick hug. 'It was good to see you again. Will you come back and see us before you leave forever?'

'I will, yes I will,' said Lavender. 'And you tell the others their Lavender's alive and happy.'

'I will.' Bramble gave her a wave and padded off into the undergrowth.

The hare was still waiting. Lavender got up onto his back, clutching the bundle of sage. '*Run now*,' she urged. '*Garden, run!*'

2

THE CURE

Fiorella was pleased to see the bundle of sage Lavender brought back, but declared that she was tired and wouldn't be doing any more work today.

'Go to bed, then,' Lavender advised. 'You can't work if you don't sleep.'

Fiorella nodded wearily. 'I don't know how much longer I can last,' she said, her voice a painful rasp. 'I would have died months ago if not for the treatments. But it's not enough to hold the disease at bay, I have to *cure* it.'

Lavender sat on the desk, still holding the fragrant sage. 'You will,' she said. She'd got into the habit of saying it at least once a day, because Fiorella needed to hear it.

'I will.' Fiorella pushed aside her untouched plate of food and stomped off to get ready for bed.

Lavender climbed onto the table and helped herself from the plate—the trip into the forest had given her a good appetite. Once Fiorella had tucked herself into bed and Lavender was sure she was asleep, she quietly wrapped up some of the leftovers and dropped them through the hole in the floorboards. The mother rat would be hungry too.

Evening drew in, and the owl flitted off through the window to hunt. Lavender watched him go. She envied him. What would it be like to fly?

She smiled wickedly to herself—one day she would find out.

For now, she climbed up the bookshelf to her own bed and settled down to sleep.

A loud clattering of pots and pans woke Lavender with a start. She sat up, blinking, and saw Fiorella, still in her nightdress, frantically taking down every single cooking pot from the cupboard above the stove. She put the last one down and ran to the cupboard where she kept her equipment and ingredients. She was looking very pale and sweaty.

Lavender picked up her hat and pulled it on. 'What are you doing?'

Fiorella stopped and looked at her. She was grinning wildly. 'I've done it,' she said. 'I found it!'

Lavender leaped out of bed. 'The cure?' she said. 'You found the cure?'

The human took in a deep breath—there was no hint of a rattle or a wheeze. 'Yes! At last—and it was so obvious! I wasn't meant to *drink* it—it worked when I *breathed* it!'

Lavender blinked in disbelief. 'You're better?'

'Yes!' And then, incredibly, Fiorella scooped up the gnome and hugged her.

Lavender made a show of trying to wriggle out of her grip—

though she was actually startled—and laughed. 'I said you'd do it!'

Fiorella quickly put her down again. 'There's no time to lose,' she said. 'I have to make as much of it as possible and write down the exact procedure.'

'Let me help,' said Lavender. 'What can I do?'

'I need more sage,' said Fiorella. 'And other herbs as well. But this time we can get them together. You can help me find them.'

'I will!'

They went into Bluedell Forest together, as they'd done before when Fiorella was stronger, and with Lavender's help the human quickly tracked down all the herbs she needed. Lavender rode in the basket looped over Fiorella's arm, which soon filled up with different kinds of leaf, flower, root, and fungus.

'All of them should be found in Vaporcitta,' said Fiorella. 'In my old garden there, among other places, and thank the Pantheon for that.'

'So once the other humans know what the cure is, they can make it themselves,' said Lavender.

Fiorella brushed a strand of dark brown hair away from her cheek. 'Just so. But before we leave, we should make plenty of it to take with us. A day should be long enough.' She smiled and took another deep, clear breath. 'Aaah, I haven't felt this energetic in months.'

'And tomorrow I could see the big city?' Lavender suggested.

'Oh no, not tomorrow. It will take us at least a week to get there, even with my steam carriage.'

'Oh.' Lavender was crestfallen, but only for a moment. They were still going.

Back at the house Lavender helped prepare the herbs, chopping them finely and tossing them into the pots when Fiorella told her to. The owl, Hedge, was used to this kind of thing and only hooted softly to show his offence.

Fiorella worked hard, almost frantically, shouting instructions to Lavender and scribbling notes on a scrap of paper. She wouldn't even stop to eat. But it was worth it; by evening they had twelve gently steaming pots of the cure and Fiorella had written a final version of the recipe. Finally, she set to work bottling the medicine, ladling it into everything from a jam jar to an empty eye-drop bottle so small Lavender could carry it.

Now, at last, Fiorella let herself rest. She and Lavender shared a meal, while Fiorella carefully copied out the recipe several times, just in case the first copy was lost.

'There,' she said at last. 'Done. Now we can get some sleep, and in the morning we'll go. I should check on my carriage. It probably needs some adjustment after all this time.'

Lavender chewed on a piece of cheese, too excited to feel tired. 'Finally, it's all done,' she said. 'I hope this isn't a dream.'

Fiorella laughed and went outside. Alone, Lavender finished eating and thought of the mother rat. She should leave her more food and maybe tell her the owner of the house was leaving. That would be a good thing since Fiorella wouldn't be there to worry about noises under the floorboards, but a bad thing because there wouldn't be any food. Though the garden would still be there, and maybe the food growing there would last long enough for the pups to grow up.

Over on his perch, Hedge ruffled his feathers and started to preen, getting ready to fly off and hunt. Lavender wondered what would happen to him. He was Fiorella's pet, after all, so maybe he'd come with them, though she didn't like the idea of seeing him in a cage again. It made him unhappy.

Hedge finished preening while Lavender was busy gathering up some food. He hopped onto the windowsill, and then stopped. He peered into the darkness, and Lavender tensed. Something wasn't right. She dropped the food and moved closer to him, along the edge of the table. '*What wrong?*' she clicked. '*Danger wrong?*'

Hedge ruffled his wings. '*Danger wrong,*' he hooted. '*Fly—*'

He leaned forward, about to launch himself from the window to safety, when a sudden loud bang shattered the stillness. The window slammed shut, glass shattering, and Hedge screeched and fluttered away. Lavender yelped in fright and started to run, but at that moment the door wrenched open and Fiorella burst in. She shoved the door closed behind her and locked it, then pressed her back to it. 'Lavender!'

Lavender hurried over. 'What is it? What's happening?'

The human's pale brown face was now nearly as pale as Lavender's. 'Kobolds,' she said. 'A pack of them—they have the house surrounded.'

Lavender's stomach dropped into her shoes. 'Kobolds?'

Fiorella ran toward the bench where the precious bottles of medicine stood in neat rows. She picked up a bag and stuffed them inside, hiding some in her pockets, along with the copies of the recipe. 'We have to go,' she said. 'We have to go *now*.'

Lavender pulled her hat off and twisted it in her hands—her heart was pattering faster than a mouse's. 'What should I do?' she said stupidly. 'What should I do?'

Fiorella stopped, looking at her, and then she nodded

sharply and snatched up the smallest bottle of all. She picked up the last copy of the recipe and wrapped it around the bottle, tying it in place with a piece of string.

'Here.' She held it out. 'Take it. Take it and—'

Something hit the door. Lavender heard a scrabbling of claws, and a deep snarling. She shrieked.

'Take it!' Fiorella was shouting now. 'Take it and get out of here. Hurry!'

Lavender snatched the bundle and stuffed it into her jerkin. There were more sounds outside now, claws tapping on the windows. A huge shaggy paw reached in through the broken window, gripping the frame and wrenching the whole thing out. Hedge fluttered around randomly, desperately searching for an escape route. The door shook.

Fiorella snatched up the knife she had used to cut herbs. Her hand was shaking. 'Get out of here, Lavender,' she said. 'Go to Vaporcitta, find the Chancellor, give him the cure. Please!'

'I will—' Lavender began, but at that moment the door finally gave in. It broke apart, the pieces crashing to the floor, and the kobolds surged in.

They were nothing like the picture in the book. Pictures were never that big, that hairy, that foul smelling.

Pictures were never that terrifying.

The first of them threw itself at Fiorella, snarling. Her knife flashed and the creature fell back, blood wetting its fur. But Lavender had no time to do anything more than flinch at the sight. A second kobold had already spotted her. It made a grab for her, but Lavender dodged it and ran, and in that panicked instant, she knew what to do.

'*Owl!*' she screeched. '*Friend owl! Fly now, we fly!*'

With that she leaped off the table and onto the floor,

between the kobold's legs and away. It stumbled after her, but it didn't get far. Something big flashed between them, and Lavender felt the talons catch in her jerkin. She reached up and caught hold of the owl's legs, and Hedge picked her up and shot out through the remains of the door and into the night.

3

THE GNOME WHO FLEW

Hedge was too panicked to fly anywhere in particular. He reached the forest and landed on a high branch, dropping Lavender in the process. She caught hold of the owl's perch and pulled herself up, her head spinning.

Clinging on tightly, she looked down. 'Deep Spirit, we're sitting on top of the world,' she breathed.

She had thought the top of Fiorella's bookshelf was high, but that was nothing compared to this. The ground was so far down she could barely see it. Not even a human could reach this high. And if she fell... if she fell she would die. The sudden certainty crossed her mind, and her stomach lurched as if she'd swallowed a grasshopper.

Hedge preened his wings again, calming himself.

'*Stay,*' Lavender told him quickly. '*Friend owl, stay.*' If he flew off now, she would be done for.

To her great relief, Hedge adjusted his grip on the branch and said, '*Stay, friend gnome.*'

Lavender breathed deeply and checked that the cure was still safe inside her jerkin. It was. And now it was the only bottle left—she was sure of that. What the kobolds couldn't eat, they would destroy.

Bizarrely, ridiculously, her first thought was of the mother rat and her pups. Would the kobolds find them? Would they pull up the floorboards and eat the helpless pups and their poor, brave mother?

'Fiorella,' she mumbled to herself. 'They killed her. They're eating her.'

There was no reply from Hedge. He might not have understood even if she'd been speaking his language. To an owl, all other lives were meaningless unless they were their own, or the lives of their young.

But he could still help her.

Lavender stood up, balancing carefully on the branch and forcing herself not to look down. 'We have to go to Vaporcitta,' she said, still talking to herself. 'We have to take the cure there. That's what Fiorella wanted. And...' she hesitated. 'I can't walk there, so... I have to fly.'

Hedge clicked his beak—he was already getting restless.

Lavender stroked his wing. *'Fly?'* she suggested. *'Fly home?'*

'Home?' Hedge repeated.

'Old, old home,' said Lavender. *'Hatch home.'* She knew the owl had hatched in Vaporcitta and lived there for most of his life. Surely, like all birds, he remembered it.

'Hatch home,' said Hedge, seeming to understand her meaning. He shuffled his talons. *'Home, fly home, friend gnome.'*

He didn't like it much when Lavender climbed onto his back, but he let her do it. She lay flat between his wings, arms wrapped around his neck, and waited. She felt the owl tense beneath her, and then they were in the sky, nothing between her and the ground but him.

Lavender held on tightly, eyes closed, trying not to think about what would happen if she lost her grip, or if Hedge lost his balance and threw her off. How far could he fly with her weighing him down? But what other choice did she have? Only he could know the way to the human capital, and there was no time left to lose.

Hedge didn't exactly take instructions from her, but he did seem to know what he was doing. He reached the river and flew along it, wings silent in the night. Lavender held on, still not daring to relax her grip. The air was cold up here, and the wind kept trying to steal her hat. *Wind sprites*, she thought, but she couldn't spare a hand to pull it back down. If she lost it, she lost it.

Time passed, and she finally risked opening her eyes. The wind stung, and her eyes watered unbearably. Even if her eyesight had been clear, she wouldn't have been able to see much more than the back of Hedge's neck and a faint glimmer of stars. But she carefully lifted her head to peer down through the gap between the owl's neck and wing and glimpsed the river, shining silver in the moonlight. Everything beyond it was a dark blur.

After that she didn't try to look again. Once was enough, and she wouldn't be able to help him navigate anyway.

Eventually she slipped into a shallow doze.

A sudden lurch beneath her woke her up with a horrible start. Still holding on tightly, she blinked and realised there was light now. Only faint, but there. Dawn was coming.

So was the ground. Hedge was flying downward. Lavender leaned back as his head tilted, afraid she would go straight over it, but in fact he landed gently, touching down on a tiled rooftop.

Lavender fell off his back, and nearly fell a lot further than that, but she caught hold of the edge of a tile and pulled herself back up. She sat down by Hedge, breathing hard. Her stomach had gone all fluttery again.

As for Hedge, he just looked tired. He huddled on his perch and went to sleep without a word, leaving Lavender to try to discover just where they were. She was on a rooftop, that was obvious, but it couldn't be Fiorella's. In fact, she realised, there were other rooftops here too. She looked around, amazed. More houses! At least... twelve of them, all with tiled roofs. And there was the river—no, it was a lake now, bigger than she had ever imagined.

Despite everything, Lavender laughed aloud. 'It's so big! It's all so big!'

She looked down into the streets between the houses. Humans walked by. Not many of them, but though Fiorella was the only human she had ever seen, she knew these must be humans as well. They were big and tall like her, though not so nicely dressed. One of them—she thought it might be a man— looked up and saw Hedge. He also saw Lavender.

'Look!' he said in a loud voice. 'Look, there's a gnome on the roof!'

Others looked up, too, with surprised expressions. 'That's a gnome,' someone else said.

Lavender waved at them. 'Hello,' she shouted. 'I'm Lavender!'

The humans started to laugh and nudge each other. 'That's

the strangest thing I've ever seen,' the first man said. 'A gnome on a roof! How did you get up there?'

'I flew!' said Lavender.

The man came closer. 'Can you come down?'

Lavender looked around. She risked shuffling forward, but nervousness stopped her. If she lost her footing, she would go sliding off the roof. 'I don't think I can,' she said honestly. 'It's too high!'

The humans talked among themselves for a moment, before the man said, 'Wait here and I'll find a ladder.'

Lavender waited, hugging her knees. She was cold and hungry and nervous. She couldn't let Hedge leave without her, or she would never make it to the city. But maybe these humans could help.

The man came back with a ladder and propped it against the edge of the roof. He climbed up it, and when he reached the top, he held out his hands, cupping them like a bowl. 'Here,' he said. 'Slide down to me and I'll catch you.'

Lavender clutched at her hat. 'Will you?'

'Yes, I promise. Come on!'

She glanced at Hedge. He was still asleep. Finally, she decided to risk it. She wrapped her arms around herself, protecting the bottle of medicine, and pushed forward off the roof's peak. From there she slid down the tiles on her backside for a short distance, until something caught and she twisted sideways and rolled the rest of the way, yelping in fright. The human's hands suddenly closed around her, and she came to a stop.

'There,' he said. 'You're safe.'

Lavender sat up, suddenly grinning. 'That was fun! Thank you.'

'You're welcome. Now, hold still and I'll carry you down the ladder.'

'Easy!' Lavender wriggled out of his grip, climbed down his arm, and sat down on his shoulder, holding onto his ear. 'Now we can go.'

The man laughed and slid down the ladder, hitting the ground with a thump. The onlookers, all very amused, applauded him.

Lavender stood up on his shoulder. 'Hello,' she said again. 'I'm Lavender of Bluedell.'

'That's a long way away,' her rescuer said, looking sideways at her. 'How did you come to be so far from home, Lavender? I didn't think gnomes ever travelled.'

'I'm a special gnome,' Lavender boasted. 'I can read as well as travel, because I learned from...' She trailed off and her smile faded as something twinged in her chest.

'You can read?' said another human—a woman.

Lavender nodded. 'A human called Fiorella taught me how. But now she's gone. Kobolds ate her.'

The humans all grimaced. 'Those monsters,' a man muttered.

'But now I'm on a journey,' Lavender told him. 'With Hedge.' She pointed up to him.

'You mean you were riding on that owl?' asked the man who had rescued her.

Lavender nodded. 'What's your name?'

'I'm Figaro,' he said. 'And this is Como Village. Where are you going?'

'Fiorella found the cure to the plague, and I've got it,' Lavender said without a moment's hesitation. 'I'm taking it to Vaporcitta so I can give it to the Chancellor.'

Every human froze. '*What?*' said Figaro.

Lavender took the little bottle out of her jerkin and held it up. 'This is the medicine,' she said.

Figaro lifted her down off his shoulder and let her stand on his open palm. 'You have... that can cure the plague?'

'Yes,' said Lavender. 'It fixed Fiorella.'

The humans started to talk in loud, excited voices. 'A cure? A cure for the plague?'

'That's right,' said Lavender. She pulled the recipe free and put it back in her jerkin, then showed them the little bottle and the yellow liquid inside. 'You have to make it hot and breathe in the smoke,' she told them.

The woman who had spoken before came forward, holding out a hand. 'Please,' she said. 'My husband is sick. Please, let me have it.'

Lavender hesitated. 'But... Fiorella said to give it to the Chancellor. And the recipe for making more of it.'

'Please!' the woman said again. 'Please, I need—'

Lavender quickly put the bottle away. 'I shouldn't.'

The woman gave a cry of despair and made a grab for her. But Figaro pushed her back. 'Stop!'

'We have to have it,' someone else yelled. 'Take it from her!'

Lavender pressed herself against Figaro's chest. 'I have to give it to—'

Figaro held up his free hand. 'Wait,' he said. 'Stop. Every-one, be quiet.'

The shouting died down.

'Lavender,' Figaro exclaimed. 'Did you say you have the recipe? Instructions on how to make it?'

'Yes, it's here.'

'Then can you give us that? Tell us how to make it?'

'Yes!' said Lavender. 'I can read it to you.'

'But what if we don't have the ingredients?'

'I can find them,' said Lavender. 'They're just herbs. I helped Fiorella find them.'

People cheered.

'We're saved!' a man cried.

'Thank you so much, Lavender,' said Figaro. 'How can we ever repay you?'

Lavender bit her lip. 'Um, I'm hungry. And Hedge needs food too.'

Lavender was tired, too, but she didn't get any rest that day. She sat on the table in Figaro's house, and the people listened eagerly while she read out the recipe to them.

'I know where to find some split leaf sage,' the woman with the sick husband said at once. 'And rosemary.'

'I can find the gnome-hat flowers,' said someone else.

In moments they had hurried away to gather what they needed, while Figaro and two others collected pots and put them on the stove. Lavender watched as she ate some fresh bread and a slice of apple as long as her arm.

After a few hours—she could tell by the clock on the wall— all the ingredients had been gathered, and Lavender read out the instructions explaining what to do with them. Soon half a dozen pots were bubbling away, and when the medicine was ready, the people who had been waiting came forward, pushing to be at the front, holding out pots and jars. They took those away, running back to their homes, and Lavender watched them go, thinking Fiorella would be happy.

'How far is it to Vaporcitta?' she asked Figaro, who was looking exhausted but smiling.

'A week on foot,' he said. 'Or two days by steam carriage. I don't know how long it would take if you were flying.'

'Flying is fast,' Lavender agreed.

'But if that owl goes without you, I can find you another bird,' said Figaro. 'Or I can take you to the city myself.'

'Do you have a steam carriage?'

'Yes. It doesn't work very well, but we could use it,' said Figaro.

'Thank you!' said Lavender.

He shook his head. 'No, don't thank me. We should be thanking you. If this cure works, then you saved a hundred people by coming here today.'

Lavender grinned. 'I wonder how many people in Vaporcitta are sick.'

'I don't know,' said Figaro. 'Thousands, probably.' He grimaced. 'So many people dying... The elves have been trying to help us, but they couldn't find the cure. So odd that it would be a human who found it.'

'Elves!' Lavender's interest perked up at once—she'd never seen an elf before. 'Fiorella's book says they can live for a thousand years!'

'That's what I heard,' said Figaro. He passed her another slice of apple. 'Some people say they never die at all—that they're immortal.'

'They must know lots,' said Lavender. 'Maybe even more than Fiorella did.'

'They're the wisest people in Hylah,' said Figaro. He paused. 'How long do gnomes live? Do you mind telling me?'

Lavender munched the slice of apple; all that flying and talking had given her a big appetite. 'The big old patriarch in Bluedell was two hundred and seventeen years under this earth,' she said, slipping back into gnomish speech habits. 'He's the oldest of all. Me, I'm only forty.' She glanced up from her meal. 'How long do humans live, then?'

Figaro scratched his head. 'You're older than I am! We only live to about sixty—sometimes more, but usually less.'

Lavender frowned. 'That's sad. You hardly live any time at all.'

'But now, thanks to you and Fiorella, some of us will live longer than we would have otherwise.'

Lavender lost her frown. 'So you will!'

4

VAPORCITTA

The human city stank.

Lyell sat on the balcony of the room the Chancellor had provided for him and looked down grimly on the rooftops —not that they were easy to see. A thick layer of smoke covered everything. It rose from the stacks of the factories, and the funnels of the train that carried goods from places as far away as Fivrath. Most of Vaporcitta's coal supplies had come from there.

And it stank. Not just of smoke, but of unwashed human bodies, rotting food, bad water.

Corpses.

Not far from the Chancellor's hall, Lyell could see a steam carriage slowly trundling along. Its open back was loaded with dead bodies. Humans, slumped on top of each other, piled carelessly like a heap of old cloth. The carriage shuddered to a stop, and a man jumped down and picked up another body lying in the street. Protected by a breathing mask and gauntlets, he heaved it onto the pile and the carriage went on its way, heading for a nearby factory that Lyell knew had been converted into a crematorium. There was no way of knowing just how many bodies had been burned there.

Lyell knew he couldn't catch the plague. But still he felt sick.

He turned away from the sight and went back inside, where the air was slightly cleaner. There was a bowl of fruit on the table, but he didn't want to eat any of it. It was human grown and contaminated by their pollution.

Disgusted, Lyell sat down. The human-sized chair was too small for him, but he could manage. Beside the fruit bowl, the sprout sat in its pot, grown larger now. He stroked one with his fingertip and felt a little better. At least something here was still clean and pure, if only because he had used his magic to keep it in good health.

He wished he could go home. Anything to be away from this terrible place. More than that, he wished Agafya was there, if only he could bear to look her in the face again. But she couldn't know what he had done. Nobody could.

He buried his face in his hands and let his shoulders slump. Here, while he was alone, he could let his feelings show. Here, for a little time, he could be himself.

A noise from the table made him look up sharply. The plant he had brought with him was moving. Before his eyes, a new leaf began to sprout. It was fresh and green, and as it grew larger, patterns appeared on its surface, woven into the veins. Lyell leaned in close and examined them. To anyone else they would have been elegant but meaningless, but to him they were words. Only two of them this time.

Any news?

Lyell took the leaf between his hands and let his magic meld with it. The plant responded at once. He could feel the life in it; the sap flowing up its stem. Far away, back in his home, the Blackfletch tree would sprout a new leaf of its own, one marked with his reply.

More deaths. City decimated. No cure.

There was no answer, but he knew Lord Skytree would have seen it. He could picture the other elf nodding to himself and turning away, satisfied for the time being. But he would be expecting a proper report later. Lyell wasn't looking forward to that—not only because he had nothing real to say for the moment, but also because it would take a lot of energy and being here had left him feeling tired and vulnerable.

He glanced up. Evening was drawing in, which was not a good sign. Soon there would be even more smoke in the air, as the humans lit their night-time fires. Finally giving up, he went to close the glass doors that led onto the balcony and went into the bedroom to take his medicine. It soothed his lungs and his stomach and left him feeling able to eat without wanting to throw up. He didn't like human food very much, but it would have to do.

Afterward, when he had eaten and cleaned his teeth with a special paste he had brought with him, he stretched out on the bed and comforted himself with thoughts of Agafya as he drifted off to sleep.

A loud knocking woke him up. He sat up sharply, instantly alert. It was still dark, and he got up and padded out into the sitting room, where the door to his quarters was.

'Who is it?'

'My Lord Blackfletch!' The human voice from outside was muffled, but excited. 'There's news!'

Lyell hadn't bothered to undress before going to bed. He

opened the door, blinking uncomfortably in the light from the hallway. 'What news?'

The human, a man, was grinning. 'My Lord, something wonderful has happened. There is a cure!'

Lyell started. 'A cure?'

'Yes, my Lord—a messenger came to us from the countryside. She has the cure. The Chancellor asked me to tell you at once.'

'Show me the way,' Lyell said sharply.

The man nodded and hurried away, and Lyell strode after him, easily able to keep up with his longer legs. Along the way, he smoothed down his hair and carefully tucked it behind his pointed ears, then straightened his leaf-shaped tunic. His heart was pounding. A cure? Now? He touched the black arrowhead pendant he wore and muttered a quick prayer in his own language. This would change everything.

The messenger brought him to the Chancellor's own quarters, which were larger than Lyell's. Paintings hung on the walls, most of them showing pictures of human machinery. The Chancellor himself was there in the sitting room, looking tousled but excited. He was middle-aged by human standards, brown-haired, and still wearing his nightshirt. Cogwheel symbols had been tattooed on his forehead, cheek, and the side of his neck. Status symbols, Lyell knew.

He greeted Lyell with a smile and a deep bow. 'My Lord Blackfletch. I'm sorry to wake you at this hour, but...'

'Are you an elf?' a small voice piped up.

Lyell looked down at the table and saw the little figure standing on it. A female gnome. She was pale-skinned, as gnomes generally were, and had rough brown hair peeking out from under a little leather cap. By the look of her she was a country gnome—city dwelling members of her race wore bright colours to avoid being stepped on. This one was holding a tiny glass bottle full of yellow liquid and a folded piece of paper.

Lyell frowned at her. 'I am,' he said. 'And you are?'

'I'm...' The gnome paused. 'Call me Vender. I'm from Bluedell. What's your name?'

The Chancellor flushed, but Lyell couldn't hold back the hint of a smile. 'I am Lord Lyell Blackfletch, ambassador for Lord Brinu Skytree. And what brings you to Vaporcitta, Vender?'

'I have the cure,' the gnome said loudly, or as loudly as someone her size could. She held up the bottle. 'I brought it here to give to the Chancellor.'

The Chancellor sat down to speak to her. 'And you say my sister made it?'

The gnome frowned. 'Her name was Fiorella Agano.'

'And mine is Albano Agano,' said the Chancellor. 'Fiorella is my younger sister.'

Vender's big eyes widened. 'Oh!'

Lyell sat down too. In spite of the situation, he was still amused. 'And you say Fiorella found the cure?'

'Yes, in Bluedell,' said Vender. 'I helped her. But then the kobolds came, and...'

The Chancellor winced. 'No... Did my sister...?'

'She died,' the gnome said solemnly. 'But she asked me to come here and bring you the cure.'

The Chancellor rubbed his eyes. 'I see. So you flew here.'

'Yes, with Hedge. Here.' Vender held out the cure. 'It's yours. It works.'

The Chancellor took it. 'Thank you, Vender.'

Lyell leaned forward. 'Are you certain it works, Vender? Have you seen it work?'

'Yes, it does,' said Vender. 'I went to Como, and I showed

the recipe to Figaro. They made the cure and healed everyone who was sick. And it made Fiorella better too.' She handed the recipe to the Chancellor. 'Here, you'll need this.'

Lyell stayed impassive, though his mind was racing.

The Chancellor, on the other hand, was beaming. 'Thank you so much, Vender. You don't know what this means to me—to all of us. My sister would have been proud of you. You came all this way to save human lives, when you aren't even one of us. You did it out of the goodness of your heart.'

'It was what Fiorella wanted,' Vender said simply.

'You are a hero now, Vender,' said the Chancellor. 'Soon you'll have earned the gratitude of every man and woman in the city. If there is anything we can offer you in return, anything at all... I'll give you anything that's in my power to give. I promise.'

'You have done well,' Lyell agreed. He stood up abruptly. 'If you will excuse me, I must report this at once.'

'Please do,' said the Chancellor. 'And thank you too, my Lord, for all your help so far. Please pass on my thanks to Lord Skytree.'

'I will.'

The moment he was alone in his quarters, Lyell sat down and sent his message. It took some time, though he kept it short and to the point.

Cure found. Sample and recipe brought. Proven to work. Action?

The reply came quickly, and it was exactly what he had expected it to be.

Destroy cure immediately. Kill one who brought it. Immediately.

As Lord Blackfletch left, Lavender took off her hat and scratched her head. So *that* was what an elf looked like. Even taller than a human, with weird golden eyes and skin the colour of wood. There had been a vine tattoo wrapped around his arm, which she thought looked interesting. Maybe she could have a tattoo like that.

'He was nice,' she said, half to herself.

'Lyell Blackfletch has been a great help to us,' said the Chancellor. 'He helped our doctors and chemists search for the cure here in Vaporcitta and sent for rare herbs from Silverwood.'

'Did the elves try to help the dwarves as well?' asked Lavender.

'Yes, Lyell was with them in Fivrath before he came here.'

'But the dwarves all died, didn't they?' said Lavender.

'I think so, Vender,' said the Chancellor. 'If there were any survivors, they must have fled.'

Lavender smiled internally at the sound of her new name. 'At least that won't happen to you now.'

'I hope not,' said the Chancellor. 'Now, it's time for you to name your reward, if you have one in mind.' He waved to the other human who was standing over by the door, and he came over at once.

While Lavender thought, the Chancellor pressed the recipe into the man's hand. 'Take this to the Chemical Institute immediately. Wake everyone up—*everyone*. Have it copied as many times as you can and tell them to start work at once. I don't want a moment's delay—understand?'

The man nodded. 'I won't let you down.' He ran out of the room.

Lavender watched him go. 'I want to see the city,' she said finally.

'Is that all?' The Chancellor looked amused.

Lavender paused. What *did* she want? To see things. To learn things.

'I want to learn,' she said aloud. 'Fiorella taught me a lot, but I want to learn more.'

'I could arrange a tutor for you,' the Chancellor suggested. 'And you could have full access to my library. And if you want to see the city, I can find a guide for you.'

'Yes, please!' said Lavender. 'I want to ask Lord Blackfletch if I can see Silverwood.'

'You can ask him, but I doubt he would give you permission,' said the Chancellor. 'Very few people are ever allowed into Silverwood.'

Lavender wasn't intimidated. 'I'll ask him.'

'Very well, but ask him tomorrow. It wouldn't be polite to wake him up again.'

'I won't,' Lavender promised.

5

SALAMANDER

Vender spent that night on the Chancellor's couch, more than happy to sleep at last. She hadn't had much sleep at all on her way to the city. Hedge had flown all night, and often when he landed it was on a tree branch, or somewhere else too uncomfortable and dangerous for sleeping. She'd had to do her best. Now, though, she had this lovely soft thing to rest on, which she gladly did, her hat pulled down over her eyes.

The sound of shouting woke her up. She sat up, hat falling off, and looked around in confusion. Her back was aching, and the sound of shouting was coming from behind the door. A moment later someone started to bang on it, so hard it was as if they wanted to break it down.

Kobolds!

Vender leaped up, clutching her hat, and had just started to look for a hiding place when she realised she could hear what the shouters were saying. 'Chancellor! *Chancellor!*'

The Chancellor came running, stumbling as he tried to

pull on a dressing-gown, and wrenched the door open. 'What? What is it?'

The woman on the other side was almost as pale as Vender. 'Chancellor! My Lord—it's gone! The cure!'

The Chancellor stiffened. 'What?'

'It's...' The woman wrung her hands. 'Biagio—he never made it to the plant. We found him unconscious in the street. The cure was gone.'

'Oh no!' said Vender.

The Chancellor swore. 'Is Biagio all right? Did he say anything?'

'He's awake now, but he doesn't know anything. Someone hit him from behind.'

'We have to get it back!' Vender yelled. 'We have to find it!'

The Chancellor turned to her. 'Can you remember it?' he asked sharply. 'The recipe—can you remember what it was?'

'Um.' Vender twisted her hat between her hands. 'Um... there was split leaf sage, and gnome-hat blooms, and rosemary, but... I can't remember how it goes together. Everything had to be in the right order, and the right heat.'

'Try,' he said. 'Tell us as much as you can remember, and we'll write it down.'

'Okay.' Vender jumped onto the table, and the Chancellor fetched a piece of paper and a pen. Before he sat down, he turned to the woman. 'Put out the word. I want the city searched from top to bottom. Whoever finds the thief and brings the cure back will be rewarded. Anyone who helps that thief will be executed.'

The woman nodded and ran away.

'Now.' The Chancellor picked up his pen. 'Tell me everything, Vender.'

Vender closed her eyes to help herself remember and told

him as much of the recipe as she could remember. The ingredients, and the amounts that should be used. The Chancellor scribbled everything down.

'Good,' he said. 'Very good. If we have part of it, then we should be able to recreate it with some work. But who knows how many will die before we succeed.'

'I'll look for it,' said Vender. 'I could find the cure.'

The Chancellor shook his head. 'You've done enough, Vender. You've earned the right to some rest. Let us find it. My soldiers know what to do. You can do what you like for the time being. But if you remember anything more, please tell me at once.'

'I will,' said Vender. She scratched her ear. 'Maybe I can see Lord Blackfletch now. He could help us.'

'Go and see him then, if you like,' said the Chancellor. 'I'll send someone to show you to his room. But remember to be polite.'

'I'm not scared of him,' said Vender. 'I like him.'

Another human showed her to the elf's door. Vender happily rode on the man's shoulder, as she had done with Fiorella many times. Human shoulders made good perches.

The human knocked on the door for her, and a moment later Lyell appeared. He was even taller than Vender remembered, and his black hair was a little messy. But he had put on a new outfit: a green shirt, with leaf shapes at the bottom and along the sleeves, and loose brown trousers. A long dagger hung from his belt.

'Hello,' said Vender. 'I came to visit you. But there's very bad news.'

The elf looked impassively at her. 'Yes?'

'Someone stole the cure,' said Vender. 'Everybody is looking for it now.'

Lyell's eyes narrowed. 'Stolen! By who?'

'They don't know,' said Vender.

Lyell glanced at the human servant. 'Perhaps you should come in. Here.' He held out a hand.

Vender stepped onto it, and Lyell nodded to the servant, dismissing him. Then he carried Vender into his room, closing the door behind them.

She jumped off his hand and onto the table, where there was a plant with strange patterns on its leaves. She inspected it with interest. 'What kind of plant is this? Is it from Silverwood?'

Lyell came over to her. 'Yes. It's a cutting from my family's tree.'

'Your family has a tree?'

Lyell sat down. He looked funny, sitting on a chair made for humans. He was too tall and had to hunch over to look at her. 'Every elvish family has a tree, or a grove of trees,' he said.

'So you carry a piece of yours with you when you go away,' said Vender. 'That's clever. Fiorella's books didn't say that. She said humans don't know much about elves really, and the Chancellor said you never let anyone into Silverwood. Well, hardly anyone. I'd let you into the tunnels at Bluedell,' she added. 'But I don't think you would fit.'

Once again, the hint of a smile showed at the corner of Lyell's mouth. 'Vender... That's an odd name for a gnome.'

'Really, it's Lavender,' she admitted. 'But I thought Vender sounded better.' She looked up at him. 'Do you think it's better?'

'It's easier to say,' said Lyell. He paused. 'But I'm not sure if it suits you.'

'Maybe I can change, then,' said Vender.

Lyell watched her for a long moment. 'How old are you, Lavender?'

'Vender,' she corrected. 'I'm forty-one. How old are *you*?'

Lyell frowned. 'That is not a polite question to ask an elf.'

'Oh.' Vender looked away quickly. 'Um... can you help us find it? The cure?'

'I doubt I would be much help,' said Lyell. 'The human soldiers can find the thief, I'm sure.'

'That's what the Chancellor said,' said Vender. She made a face. 'He didn't want me to help. But couldn't you use your elvish magic to find it?'

'Our magic does not work that way,' Lyell said shortly. He was still looking at her, his gaze very intent, as if she was a book he was reading.

'What are you doing?' Vender asked him.

Finally, Lyell said, 'Why did you come here, Vender? Why did you risk your life to bring the cure here?'

'Because Fiorella asked me to,' said Vender.

'But these are humans,' said Lyell. 'They aren't your kind. Don't you have a family of your own?'

'Yes, in Bluedell,' said Vender. 'But I always liked it better out of the tunnels. I wanted to see how far I could go. Then one day I saw Fiorella looking for herbs. The others were afraid to let her see them, but I wasn't scared, so I talked to her. I told her I knew all the herbs in the forest, so she taught me to read and talk properly so I could help her.'

'So you never wanted to go back?' asked Lyell.

Vender considered it. 'No. I don't think they want me back, really. I'm not like them.'

'You certainly aren't like any gnome I ever spoke to,' said Lyell, again with the hint of a smile.

'Can I go with you?' Vender asked abruptly. 'When you go back to Silverwood, can I go with you?'

The tiny smile disappeared. 'I think that would be a bad idea.'

'Please?' said Vender. 'I always wanted to see it.'

'No, Vender. Don't ask me.'

Vender caught the warning in his voice. 'Well,' she said, crestfallen, 'can you show me the city instead? The Chancellor promised me a guide, but... I like you.'

Lyell's fingers twitched, and he looked away.

'Please?' said Vender.

'The city is in a terrible state now, Vender,' Lyell said without looking at her. 'I don't think you know how bad. The plague is everywhere. Humans are lying dead in the street.'

Vender's face fell. 'That's terrible... If only the cure wasn't lost. But we can fix it,' she added. 'I told the Chancellor what I remembered, and he wrote it down. He says we can find the cure again in a while.'

Lyell rubbed his forehead. 'I suppose... we could visit the marketplace.'

'Yes, please!' said Vender. 'I always wanted to see a marketplace.'

'Come, then,' said Lyell. He picked up a small leather bag and slung it over his shoulder, then reached down and gently picked Vender up. He lifted her onto his shoulder, and she settled herself down, heart pattering. She was riding on an elf! She looked up at his ear, which was pointed like her own, but longer. Could that mean that gnomes and elves were related? Like cousins? No, that was a silly idea. But still... Now she had an elf for a friend, and she preferred that. She'd never really liked her cousins that much.

Lyell left the Chancellor's hall and went out into the city, Vender still riding on his shoulder. She wrinkled her nose at the smell as soon as they were in the open.

'It stinks here!'

To her surprise, Lyell said, 'It does, doesn't it? The air is so bad—no wonder the humans are sick. I would be sick myself, without my medicine.'

'You have medicine?'

'Yes, from Silverwood,' said Lyell. 'It was made from the sap of a special plant. I need to have some with me when I travel to places such as these. My lungs can't work the way they should here.'

Vender coughed. 'Maybe I need some medicine too. I feel like I could choke!'

'So do I,' said Lyell. 'Let's not go too far.'

'All right.' Despite her burning throat, Vender felt more than ready to put up with this if it meant she could see the city.

She took it in as Lyell walked down the main street, amazed. It was so much different from what she had expected. So big, so full of smoke. The walls of the buildings were so grimy she thought they had more soot on them than the inside of Fiorella's chimney. There were some humans around, but not very many, and all of them were wearing something over their faces. Some had tied strips of cloth over their mouths and noses, but others had masks covering their whole faces, with glass circles for their eyes and slits to breathe through. Most of them were wearing gloves and many of them showed no skin at all, shrouding them-selves in heavy coats, boots, and pants. They looked up at Lyell as he passed, and Vender caught the awe and fear in their eyes.

'What are they doing?' she asked. 'It's so hot. Why are they dressed up like that?'

The heat was indeed stifling, and the smoke wasn't help-ing. Lyell stifled a cough. 'They are hoping to protect them-selves from the plague.'

'Oh,' said Vender. That made sense. 'How does the plague make humans sick, then?'

'It comes in through the lungs,' said Lyell. 'One breath of a sick human's cough and the infection spreads.'

Vender saw a woman lying in the gutter and flinched. 'Is she...?'

Lyell glanced down at the body. 'I warned you.'

'But why is she just lying there?' said Vender. 'Why isn't somebody sending her to the Deep Spirit?'

'Humans don't worship the Deep Spirit,' said Lyell. 'And with so many dying here, few are left to carry the bodies away.'

Vender tried to imagine something like this happening in Bluedell but failed. 'This is so terrible. Why would someone steal the cure?'

Lyell didn't answer.

After a while, Vender spotted something ahead. She pointed. 'Is that it? The market?'

'Yes.' Lyell sped up, and a moment later they were in a quite crowded area of the city. Tables lined the street, and there were humans standing behind them, all masked. They were selling things: food, pieces of machinery, clothes, masks, and other things to protect people from the plague. But at least half the stalls Vender saw were selling bottles. Bottles of all kinds of liquid, pills, dried herbs, and powders. The nearest one had a crude sign hanging up that said 'Herbs and Tinctures! New Plague Treatments Here!'

Vender tugged on Lyell's ear. 'Look,' she said. 'They have medicine for the plague!'

'None of it works,' Lyell told her in an undertone. 'It may treat the symptoms, but the cure is not here.'

'Oh.' Vender was crestfallen. But she kept her eyes open, looking for any sign of a yellow liquid that might be Fiorella's cure. Maybe the thief was here trying to sell it.

Further along, they came across a stall stacked with cages. They were full of birds, busily chirping away, and they caught Vender's attention at once. 'Poor birds! Look at them, locked away.'

Lyell went over to the stall. 'Humans like to keep birds as pets,' he said.

'I know,' said Vender. She called out to the nearest one. *'Bird, friend bird. Not happy?'*

The bird chirped back at her. *'Gnome friend. Thirsty. Water?'*

Vender looked up at the man selling the birds. 'That bird there wants water,' she said, pointing. 'She's thirsty.'

The human looked mildly surprised. 'A gnome,' he said. 'Hello. And you...' He bowed to Lyell, saying nothing.

'She wants water,' Vender insisted.

The man nodded. 'Blackberry, get some water.'

Before Vender could ask what he was talking about, something emerged from behind the cages that made her gasp. Another gnome!

The other gnome was also female, but dressed unlike any gnome Vender had ever met. Her hat was bright red, her jerkin yellow, and her pants green. She looked up at Vender with interest. 'Country gnome, you is?'

'Yes, yes, a gnome of Bluedell,' Vender answered. 'Named Vender. But you? City gnome?'

'Yes, city,' said Blackberry. 'Many gnomes to be found here. Useful now—no plague for us!'

'No plague,' Vender agreed. 'Lucky to be gnome!'

Blackberry nodded back and bustled off to get some water for the bird. Vender took in the rest of the cages. Some of the birds here were kinds she had never seen before. And one of them wasn't a bird at all.

She blinked at the sight of it. It looked like a lizard, more than twice her size, with smooth black skin. There were lurid red markings around its eyes, and its belly was spotted with yellow. There was a webbed crest on its head, and another on its tail, and a cluster of long spines lay flat against its side.

'What is that?' Vender said in wonder.

Lyell stooped to inspect it. 'A salamander,' he said with surprise. 'I never saw one outside Fivrath before.'

'Salamander?' Vender repeated.

The human stallholder cleared his throat. 'It's a very rare specimen,' he said. 'Brought all the way from Fivrath before the plague killed the last of the dwarves.'

'What's a salamander?' Vender asked.

'A fire lizard,' Lyell said in an odd voice. 'Some call them dragons.'

The stallholder picked up a stick and prodded the salamander, which reared up and hissed. The spines on its sides suddenly moved, spreading out into two pairs of blue-webbed wings. The man prodded it again, and it spat a small fireball at him.

'Stop that!' said Vender. The man took the stick away and the salamander relaxed, though its flanks were still puffed out like an angry toad.

'Very angry,' Blackberry observed. 'Angry, angry lizard.'

'Salamander,' Vender corrected. The other gnome's speech was starting to annoy her. She addressed the salamander in the hissing reptile language. *'Lizard? Friend lizard?'*

The salamander's head came up. *'Fly,'* it hissed back. *'Fly free. Hungry. Fly!'*

'Not happy?' asked Vender.

The salamander fluttered its wings against the cage bars. *'Fly free!'* it said.

Lyell was listening. 'What is it saying?'

Vender brought her head around to look at him. 'He wants to go free,' she said. 'He doesn't like it in there. Please, can you let him out?'

'Nine hundred cogs and it's yours,' the stallholder said promptly.

Vender had never even seen a cog before. 'What's that?'

'Nine hundred,' the human repeated, with a glance at Lyell. 'That's what it costs.'

'Nine hundred is a lot of money,' Lyell said coldly.

The human coughed behind his mask. 'This is the only salamander for sale in the whole city, my Lord. And nobody goes into Fivrath anymore, so there won't be any more of them.'

'Please, can you do something, Lyell?' said Vender. 'Please?'

Lyell was silent for a while, staring at the caged salamander. The birds chirruped and fluttered their wings, and Blackberry, ignoring the entire exchange, methodically refilled their water bowls.

'Eight hundred,' Lyell said eventually. 'That is my final offer.'

'Done.' The stallholder held out a hand.

Lyell opened his bag and slowly counted out eight hundred

small golden cogwheels. They looked just like the Chancellor's tattoos: ring-shaped with square teeth. Once he had the full amount, the stallholder picked up the cage and offered it to the elf. Lyell took it.

'Thank you!' said Vender.

The salamander skittered around in its cage, smoke drifting from its nostrils. *'Free, free! Friend gnome, free!'*

'We should go back now,' Lyell said quietly. 'I've seen enough.'

6

FRIEND TAIL

Back in Lyell's sitting room, Lyell put the salamander's cage down on the table. He put Vender down beside it, and she immediately hurried over to try to open the door.

'Be careful,' Lyell warned. 'Salamanders are dangerous creatures.'

'I have to set him free,' Vender insisted.

'Talk to him first,' said Lyell. 'Calm him. I know how your gift works.' With that he sat down, chin on his hand, and waited to see what she would do.

Vender paused. She could see the rage in the salamander's eyes. Maybe it would be better to talk to it first. When she was little she had been warned about predators. They could be spoken to, but any gnome who wanted to go near one should be careful.

'*Friend,*' she hissed. '*Friend gnome. You friend salamander?*'

'*Free,*' the salamander said yet again. It clawed at the bars. '*Gnome friend, free.*'

'*Friend if free,*' Vender suggested. '*Salamander friend?*'

'*Friend if free,*' said the salamander, its tongue flicking.

Vender took hold of the hook on the cage door. *'No fire,'* she said. *'No fight. Friend.'*

'No fire,' said the salamander. *'No fight. Friend.'*

Vender lifted the hook and pulled the door open. The salamander immediately pushed it all the way open, shoving it aside with its head and slithering out onto the table. It spread its four long wings and hissed, showing rows of sharp fangs the size of a gnome dagger.

Vender quickly moved out of the way. *'Friend,'* she said. *'Gnome friend.'*

The salamander blinked like a frog. Then it lowered its head toward her. *'Friend, friend gnome. Free.'*

Vender came closer and put her hands on the creature's snout. She rubbed the smooth, hard, hot skin and scratched the head crest, which flicked up and down. The salamander's eyes closed blissfully.

'Friend,' it said again. *'Friend gnome.'*

'Vender,' said Vender. *'Friend gnome Vender. Salamander friend name?'*

The creature flicked its tail. *'Name Tail.'*

'Tail,' said Vender. *'Tail friend.'*

Tail lowered his wings. *'Fly, Vender,'* he said. *'Fly with Tail.'*

Vender smiled to herself in surprise. Above her, Lyell saw her expression. 'What is he saying?'

'He asked me to fly with him,' said Vender. 'He wants to carry me.'

'Ah,' said Lyell. 'Like the owl that brought you here?'

'No, I asked Hedge to carry me. But Tail asked me. That's special.'

'Is it?' Lyell blinked. 'How?'

'When an animal asks, that means he wants to be friends,' said Vender. 'Forever.'

Lyell put his head on one side, and then a slow smile spread over his long, solemn face—the first one she had seen on him. 'I can see how you would make friends easily, Vender,' he said. 'You are... you have so much compassion in you, and innocence. Not many people... value those things as they should.'

Tail rubbed his nose against Vender's cheek. *Friend, Vender,*' he crooned.

Vender petted him. 'Thank you, Lyell. But we're friends now too, aren't we? We are, aren't we?'

Lyell looked at her for a long time, and then he suddenly sighed and buried his face in his hands. Vender watched him, confused. 'Lyell? What's the matter?'

No answer. Lyell stayed where he was, and if he had made any sound Vender might have thought he was crying.

She went over to him, Tail following her, and reached out far enough to touch the elf's knee. 'Lyell? Are you all right?'

Lyell muttered something in a language she didn't recognise.

'Is it the cure?' said Vender. 'Are you worried they won't find it again? I'm sure they will.'

Lyell took his hands away from his face—he looked perfectly calm. 'I must go,' he said, sounding a little hoarse. 'This place... I can't stay here any longer. I must go back to Silverwood. Today.'

'Can I go with you?'

Lyell stood up. 'No. Go back to Bluedell, Vender. Stay away from this place. And stay away from me.'

7

SILVERWOOD

Lyell left the human city that afternoon, having refused the Chancellor's offer of a farewell meal, and his other offer for an escort. He would travel faster on his own.

Leaf was waiting for him not far beyond the city, on the fields by the river. There had been no need to put her into a stable, or call for her to come. She knew when she should be there to meet him. Lyell walked onto the field, carrying his few possessions in a bag on his back, and his heart lifted at the sight of her. She was drinking from the river, but raised her head to look at him, her silver eyes bright. She trotted toward him, huffing loudly through her nose.

Lyell patted her on the muzzle. 'Hello, girl. How have you been?'

She huffed again and nuzzled the side of his neck. Lyell chuckled and scratched her on the chin.

The deer grunted contentedly and lay down on her belly, legs tucked in. Lyell climbed onto her back and she stood up again, ears flicking.

'Time to go home,' Lyell told her in elvish. 'Back to Silverwood.'

She understood the command and turned to trot away along the river that would lead them home.

Lyell did not look back at Vaporcitta. He was glad to be leaving. But what lay ahead of him was not the relief he had been hoping for all this time. Lord Brinu would not be happy to see him, not at all. He had sent a message through the plant to say he was returning, but he was still doing so without permission. In all likelihood, he would be told to go back. How could he look his ruler in the face and tell him he couldn't bear it any longer? That the sight of so much suffering was more than he could take? He had left Silverwood full of steely resolve, but he was coming back to it with a mind full of doubts and weaknesses.

Maybe the best thing would be to tell Brinu the truth, or some of it. That he was compromised. Let someone else take his place. There had to be someone better. Stronger. Someone who would not have succumbed the way he had and let himself feel... compassion.

Agafya. He closed his eyes. *No, don't think of her. This all began with her. If it had not been for her...*

First Agafya and now this gnome, Vender. Two lives he should have ended, and yet he had let them go. And the cure.

'Nobody can know about this,' he muttered. 'Nobody. Otherwise...' He shuddered.

Vender watched Lyell leave, though he didn't see her, or Tail. The salamander carried her on his back, out the window of the elf's room, and the two of them flew over the city. The smoke made Vender gag, but Tail didn't seem to mind it at all. He swooped and soared, Vender clinging to his back, and spat fireballs for the sheer pleasure of it. Vender whooped, though her eyes were stinging, and Tail began to fly faster. He flew low over the river, chasing dragonflies, caught one and ate it without stopping to land, and Vender managed to catch one of the insect's long, transparent wings before it blew away. She tucked it into her jerkin and pulled on Tail's crest, encouraging him to fly upward.

He did—up past a factory that stood by the canal and then around it, dodging between the great smoke-belching chimneys. The wind blew through Vender's hair, wind sprites threatening to steal her hat again, and she laughed.

After a while, Tail flew northward away from the city, toward the fields beyond its walls. From there, Vender saw Lyell. She saw the huge deer come to meet him, and watched him ride away, and her excitement slowly turned to sadness. The elf had been so kind to her, but she had seen something in him. He was sad, she thought. Very sad. But she couldn't tell why. If only she could help him.

Finally, Tail seemed to grow tired. He flew back to the Chancellor's hall, in through the open window into Lyell's room. The cage was still there, and he landed on it. Vender hopped off and patted him on the head. *'Friend Tail—good fly!'*

Tail hissed and flicked his tail. *'Good fly! Fly more soon!'*

'Fly more!' said Vender. She stretched her aching back and checked that the dragonfly wing was still in her jerkin. It was, and she smiled because she had an idea about what to do with it. But she would need some other things. Maybe she should talk to the Chancellor. She asked Tail if he would carry her some more, and he agreed.

The humans in the hall stared in bewilderment at the sight

of them: the great black lizard padding along over the carpet, Vender sitting proudly on his back. She pointed the way to the Chancellor's chambers and found him in the sitting room with two other humans she didn't recognise. He was properly dressed now, in a long red coat with gold trimmings, and his voice was light and happy.

Tail flitted up onto the table, and Vender jumped off his back. 'Hello!' she said to the startled humans.

The Chancellor started, and then beamed. 'Vender, there you are! I was hoping to see you again—I have wonderful news!'

'The cure?' Vender guessed at once.

'Yes! It's been found! The recipe, and the bottle.'

Vender grinned in disbelief. 'Where was it? Who took it?'

'We don't know who took it,' said one of the other humans. 'But they must have changed their mind. Our chemists found it on a table in the Chemical Institute's main laboratory. They are already at work making the cure.'

Vender cheered. 'I knew they would find it! I wish Lyell was here.'

'Yes, it is a pity he had to leave,' said the Chancellor. 'But never mind. Tonight there will be a special dinner here to celebrate the cure. And you'll be the guest of honour, Vender.'

'Thank you!' she said. 'Can Tail come too?'

The third human looked at him. 'Is that... a salamander?'

'Yes,' said Vender. 'He's my friend now.' She petted Tail's shoulder.

'Isn't it amazing how gnomes can tame animals?' the human remarked to the Chancellor. 'I think it's an overlooked gift.'

Vender paused. 'What magic do humans have?'

'None,' the Chancellor said with a smile. 'We rely on technology to help us. Now, would you like to have a bath before dinner?'

Vender had her bath and was given a new set of clothes, which her hosts said had been bought from a gnome tailor in the city. It was very nice: a green jerkin, brown pants, and a red hat like the ones all the city gnomes seemed to wear. And rat leather shoes, dyed blue. Vender put them on, and Tail carried her to the big dining room where the feast soon began.

There was a lot of food, and a lot of humans. The long table had been decorated with flowers, and a special spot had been set up for Vender: a gnome-sized stool on the table, with its own table in front of it. There was even a plate, fork, and cup in her size. And, when she asked for it, someone brought a bowl of raw meat for Tail, who cooked it with fire before eating it.

The humans sat along the table, with the Chancellor at the far end, and before they were allowed to eat he made a speech.

'Today we are here to honour a hero,' he said. 'Vender of Bluedell is the reason so many lives will be saved. If she had not risked her life to come to us with my sister's cure, it is possible the whole human race would have died.' He paused. 'Many humans refuse to take Vender's people seriously, and I admit, those I have met before were simple creatures, without much curiosity about the world around them. But Vender is different. She can read, and she cares for more than her own kind. She saved this city, and we will never forget.' He held up his cup. 'To Vender! The hero of Bluedell!'

The humans lifted their own cups. 'To Vender!'

Vender blushed and kicked her heels.

'Vender,' the Chancellor went on, 'I would like to tell you this: I have given orders for a statue to be made in your honour. It will stand in the city square, and your name will be on the plinth beneath it.'

'Will Tail be in the statue as well?' asked Vender.

The humans laughed, including the Chancellor.

'If you like,' he said with a smile. 'And, as I said before, if there is anything I can offer you...'

Vender chewed on her thumbnail. 'Well... can I have some thread? And a needle? I want to make something.'

'Of course.' The Chancellor sat down, still smiling, and the feast began.

Vender ate happily and tried some of everything. There were humans there to serve the food, and one took special care of her, bringing her anything she asked for. She drank wine, which she had never tried before. She didn't like the taste very much, but it made her feel good, so she drank it anyway. There was cheese and oily bread, tomatoes and olives, hams and smoked chicken, and afterward there were fresh berries in cream. Vender loved those in particular, and she shared some cream with Tail, who lapped it up. Everyone wanted to talk to her. They asked her questions about Bluedell, and her journey to the city, and what she wanted to do next. They even asked her about Lyell and what they had talked about.

'I never saw him talk to anyone very much,' said the woman who had asked her. 'He was always very quiet and reserved. Gave very little away.'

'Elves are like that, though,' said the woman next to her.

'I don't know about the rest of them, but he was like that,' her friend agreed. 'But it sounds like he liked you a lot, Vender. I heard he even carried you on his shoulder!'

'I asked if he would show me the city, and he said yes,'

Vender said with surprise. 'We bought Tail in the marketplace. And then he said he had to go. I don't know why. We were talking, and then he got... sad. He just said nothing for a while, and then he said he had to go.'

Silence fell.

'Why was he sad?' asked a man on Vender's other side.

'I don't know,' said Vender. 'Maybe he misses his home. He said he didn't like it here very much. The air was bad for him.'

'I can understand homesickness,' remarked the first woman. 'Still... he did leave suddenly.'

Vender bit her lip. 'Do you think he's all right? He didn't even say goodbye to me, and I thought we were friends.'

'I don't think anybody could be friends with an elf, except for another elf,' said the woman.

'Well, Lyell's my friend,' Vender said firmly. 'He said he liked me, and I like him.'

'A gnome who can make an elf show his feelings,' the Chancellor murmured. 'Extraordinary.'

'I wasn't trying to,' said Vender. Tail hissed softly, and she put her hand on his head.

The humans murmured, impressed, but talking about Lyell left Vender feeling sad again.

After the feast was over she asked to see the library, an impressive room even bigger than the dining hall, lined with more books than she had ever seen in one place. A man there said he was the librarian, and he offered to bring her any book she wanted.

'I want to read about elves,' Vender told him. She had been given her needle and thread as she had asked, and while the librarian went to search the shelves she sat down and started work, attaching the dragonfly wing to her old hat, where it would protect her eyes from the wind.

The librarian came back with a stack of books. 'Which one do you want to read first?' he asked. 'We have *Secrets of Silverwood, A History of Elvenkind...*'

The titles told her nothing, so she chose the first one. The librarian opened it for her, and Vender put her sewing aside and started to read. On the first page was a beautiful picture of an elf, as big as she was. She was sitting on the back of a deer, like Lyell's, and wearing a crown of leaves. Behind her was a forest of silvery-barked trees. Underneath the picture was some writing.

Lady Ostara Skytree, first known ruler of the elves.

Vender admired the picture, then turned the page. Tail squatted beside her, and she started to talk to him, though not in his language. 'It says elves are the oldest race in Hylah, and that once the whole country was nothing but forest, and they lived in it. They can use plants to do anything they want. The Skytree family are their rulers, but there are lots of different families. The Swiftrunners, the Longspears, the—Blackfletch! Look, Lyell's family is in here! And look at the picture—that's his arrow necklace. And here... it says every family has their own tree, but the Skytrees have the biggest one. The River Wend comes from under its roots. It's the oldest tree in Hylah, and they call it the Sky Tree.'

Tail peered at her while she turned another page.

'And here,' she said, 'it says the elves fought the kobolds and drove them out of their old territories, so now they wander around the country in packs, spreading diseases. Now the elves don't come out of Silverwood very much, but the humans and dwarves re... revere them. And look, a map!' She showed it to the salamander, who moved his head around to take it all in, his tongue flicking rapidly. The whole of Hylah was there—the

River Wend, Fivrath the dwarf city, Como, Vaporcitta—and there was Silverwood, at the far end of the river.

'We could go there, Tail,' said Vender. She traced the blue line with her hand. 'Follow the river. We could fly to Silverwood and see the elves. Wouldn't Lyell be surprised to see us?'

Standing nearby, the librarian said, 'I think that would be a bad idea, Vender. The elves don't welcome visitors. Only a few have ever been allowed into Silverwood.'

Vender lifted her chin. 'I made friends with Lyell,' she said. 'I can make friends with all of them.'

8

TO THE TREE

The ride back to Silverwood passed quickly enough. Lyell's deer was strong and had plenty of endurance; her kind could walk all day and night without growing tired. Along the way they passed through Como, and the humans stopped and stared at the elf, wide-eyed. Seeing them, Lyell pulled his steed to a halt and called down to them.

'Is this Como?'

'Y-yes,' a man stammered. 'Are you... I mean...?'

Lyell suppressed a sigh. 'I am Lord Lyell Blackfletch,' he said. He patted the deer's neck. 'And this is Leaf. Tell me, have any of you met a gnome named Vender? Or Lavender?'

'We have, my Lord!' a woman said eagerly. 'She brought us the cure to the plague.'

'Then it worked?' said Lyell. 'The cure healed you?'

'Yes, my Lord. Everyone who had the plague recovered.'

Lyell's mouth tightened. 'I see.'

'She said she was going to Vaporcitta,' said a woman. 'Do... do you know if she made it, my Lord?'

'She did. I saw and spoke to her there.'

The humans cheered, and Lyell went on his way, feeling sick to his stomach. Word would spread soon enough, even into Silverwood. Soon they would know what had happened. A gnome named Vender, who had brought the cure to the plague. A cure that had not disappeared, and a gnome who was still alive to tell the tale.

When he finally saw the edges of Silverwood, he felt sicker than ever. He should go, he thought. Ride away to find Agafya and never return to his people. But he thought of Fivrath, and Vaporcitta, and all the things he had seen. So much suffering. So much death. And for what? Some mad scheme to save his own race? No, he had to do something. He had to speak up. Surely someone would listen.

Leaf went in among the trees, obviously glad to be home. Lyell leaned on her back to avoid a low-hanging branch. The ground was growing steeper here, and there was no path for them to follow. On either side, between the trunks of the graceful silverwood trees, strange plants grew. Their flowers were lurid yellow, and at their hearts were round, swollen shapes like little fruits. Nothing happened, but Lyell knew that if anyone other than an elf came this way, those swellings would have exploded in a cloud of deadly venom. As it was, he and Leaf passed them by without fear.

Gradually the guard flowers thinned out as the trees grew thicker. The canopy thickened as well, covering the ground in dappled shade. Lyell breathed deeply, savouring the scents of dry leaves and the little ferns that curled among the tree roots. They were scents he had not known in far too long.

'Home,' he murmured with a smile.

The slope grew steeper still, and he could see it above him now—the massive, looming shape of the Skytree itself. Its branches rose high above the canopy of the rest of the forest, and he could see the edges of its roots now, snaking along the banks of the river. The water was beautifully clear here, sparkling and clean. It would not know filth and corruption until it reached the human settlements.

Not much further along, as the trees began to thin once more, Lyell heard a faint rustling and two figures emerged from behind a tree. Both elves, both carrying long hunting spears. They stopped at the sight of him.

'Lyell?' said one. 'Is that you?'

Lyell slid off Leaf's back. 'Eala,' he said. 'Kiya. It's... good to see you again. How long has it been?'

'Seventeen years,' said Eala, who was about his height but with blond hair. Like Kiya, she was wearing a simple outfit made of deerskin, and her feet were bare.

'Seventeen years,' Lyell repeated to himself in a low voice. Could it really have been that long? Of course, by elvish standards it wasn't that much time, but even so... Seventeen years?

Kiya was frowning at him. 'Why are you here, Lyell? Nobody said you were coming back.'

'I chose to come back,' said Lyell. 'I need to speak to Brinu.'

'What happened?' Eala asked at once. 'Did the humans die? Have you—?'

'Not now,' Lyell said in a sharp voice. 'I must speak to Brinu, immediately.'

'I will tell him you're coming,' said Kiya. She ran away ahead of them, scattering dead leaves in her wake.

Eala stayed, and she and Lyell walked alongside each other. 'I missed you.' She touched him lightly on the arm. 'We all missed you. You look so different, Lyell.'

He looked over at her. 'Do I? How?'

'You look tired, Ill. All that human and dwarvish filth, all that bad air and water. It must have been like swimming in poison.'

'I am glad to be back here,' Lyell admitted. 'The air is so pure. But the Skytree... how is it? Is it still alive?'

Eala looked grim. 'You should see it for yourself.'

He didn't have to wait long. At the top of the slope, where the river flowed faster and louder, the forest opened up into a great clearing. And there was the Skytree, at the centre of that clearing. Its rough grey trunk was the size of the Chancellor's hall, its sides rippled as if with muscle, the massive roots arched from the ground, revealing a space beneath it where faint light shone. Over their heads the branches spread to cover the clearing, but where once they had been thick with leaves, now they were bare skeletal fingers, whose shadows were stark and grim.

Lyell saw it, and horror sank into his heart. 'The Skytree...'

'Dead,' Eala whispered. 'Dead for these past five years.'

Lyell turned on her, even as the other elves began to gather. 'Why did no one tell me?'

'Because I knew that if I did, you would lose heart and abandon your mission,' a voice answered him. It came from beneath the tree, and as Lyell turned he saw Lord Brinu Skytree emerge into the daylight.

He was short for an elf, and showing some signs of his advancing age, though they were subtle enough that only another elf would have been likely to see them. His hair was brown, tied back in a braid decorated with bone beads, and he wore a crown of silver leaves.

Lyell quickly kneeled. 'My Lord Skytree.'

Brinu nodded shortly. 'Rise, Lord Blackfletch.'

Lyell stood up. 'The tree,' he said. 'The Skytree...'

'Yes,' said Brinu. 'We did all we could, but we could not save it. Our power is not enough to fight against the corruption of the dwarves and the humans. Their poison killed the Skytree. Theirs and that of the kobolds.'

Lyell hesitated. 'My Lord...'

'Why are you here?' Brinu interrupted. 'Why have you come back here? I know the humans are still alive. If not, then the Skytree would be blooming again. You left Vaporcitta while your task was incomplete.'

'Yes, I did,' said Lyell. Around him the others started to mutter. More were arriving now, coming out of the forest and into the clearing, all staring at him. Lyell quietly patted Leaf on the nose and murmured to her to go. The deer huffed and walked away into the trees.

'Lyell, why?' asked Eala. 'Why did you come back here?'

'Did you destroy it?' asked Brinu. 'The cure? And the one who brought it—did you kill him?'

Lyell hesitated for only a moment before telling the lie he had prepared. 'I tried,' he said. 'But I was too late. I destroyed the cure, but before I could kill the one who brought it she had already given the recipe to the humans. She remembered it, and they wrote it down. The cure was rediscovered. The plague will end soon.'

Silence fell.

'Then why did you not stay?' said Brinu. 'Why did you not send me a message? A new disease could easily have been prepared.'

'My Lord, I—'

'You were given orders, Lyell,' said Brinu. 'You were not allowed to return here until the cleansing of the land was complete. That was your mission, and you were honoured to have it. You *asked* to be the one to go.'

'I did, I know,' said Lyell. 'But I... my Lord, I'm sorry, but I must... I must refuse. I have no more will to continue. The task was too much for me.'

There was a murmuring from the others.

'I know it is hard, being forced to live among those lesser creatures,' said Brinu. 'But it must be done. Go back, Lyell. They trust you now. I will give you a new disease to take with you, and we have a baby kobold nearly old enough to leave. Take it to the city and release it.'

'No,' said Lyell. 'I'm sorry, but I can't.'

'Give him some time, Brinu,' another elf put in as Brinu started to speak. 'Look at him; you can see how tired he is. The subcreatures have made him ill. Let him rest. You ask too much of him.'

'There is no sacrifice too great to save the Skytree,' Brinu said stonily. 'You were prepared to lay down your life for it and your people, Lyell. Has that not changed?'

Lyell hesitated. He knew how dangerous this would be. But he had to say it. He must. For Agafya's sake. 'My Lord,' he said. 'I... I would die for my people, and for the Skytree. But... but I cannot do this anymore. I cannot stand by and watch. I have seen horrors... death and misery, the fall of civilisations almost as old as ours. And I... I no longer believe that what we are doing is right.' He shook his head. 'No. It is wrong. What we are doing is wrong... evil.'

Sharp gasps rose from the crowd. Brinu's eyes widened.

Lyell braced himself and spoke on, louder this time. 'This is evil,' he said again. 'You haven't seen them, but I have. I met so many people, and they were good and kind. They wanted to live as much as we do, and I had to watch them die. And I knew I could save them, but I did nothing. Seventy years, and I did nothing but encourage it. I stopped them from curing themselves, I pushed them to fight each other, I murdered people who trusted me. And for what?'

'Your whole family is dead because of them!' Eala shouted. 'They poisoned them, and the Skytree. We are *dying* because those creatures came into Hylah.'

'Then maybe it was meant to be,' said Lyell. 'Maybe our time is ending. But this... this is murder. Find someone else to take my place if you must. I want no more part in it.'

The others there started to shout at him, hurling abuse. 'Coward! Traitor!'

Lyell did not flinch. 'I would rather let the Skytree die than have any more part in this,' he said quietly. 'I would rather die myself.'

Brinu's face darkened. 'Did you do this on purpose?' he asked. 'Did you let the cure go deliberately?'

'I...' Lyell paused, but his hesitation was enough.

'You did, didn't you?' said Brinu. 'You let the humans keep the cure. You let the one who brought it escape.'

'I did not—' Lyell began.

Brinu's look grew even grimmer than before. 'I see how it is,' he said. 'Now I see, though I would never want to believe it. You took pity on them. You chose them over your own kind. That makes you a traitor.'

'No,' said Lyell. 'I would never—'

A rock hit him in the back of the head, and he stumbled and gasped.

'Kill him!' someone shouted. 'Kill the traitor!'

Lyell drew his dagger and backed away. His head was throbbing. 'Stop!' he said. 'You don't understand, you didn't see—'

'Take him,' Brinu said sharply. 'Now.'

The others closed in on him. Lyell turned and ran, shoving

Kiya out of his way, but it was too late. Something hit him in the back of the knee, and he fell forward, the dagger flying out of his hand. Before he could get up, his arms had been twisted behind his back, and three elves dragged him away, back to where Brinu waited. Lyell struggled, shouting at them to stop, to see sense, but they only pulled him upright and forced him to kneel in front of his ruler.

Lyell looked up at him. 'Please, don't,' he said. 'Banish me if you must. I would be happy to choose exile, believe me. There's nothing here for me anymore. I know that now.'

Brinu's look toward him was full of contempt. 'I thought better of you than this, Lyell,' he said. 'I truly did. But now I can see the corruption of the lesser races has infected even you. I will find a replacement soon enough. But as for you... you must be punished for what you have done.' He nodded to the elves holding him. 'Take him out of my sight. Give him to the tree. Do it now.'

Hot terror poured into Lyell's stomach. 'No,' he said. 'No! Please!'

But his captors only hauled him to his feet and took him away, forcing him to walk between them, away from the dead Skytree and the stares of those who had once been his friends.

'You have to stop this, Brinu!' he shouted. 'Killing them won't save us. This is wrong and you know it!'

The elf on his left side hit him hard in the head, and Lyell fell silent, but he kept on struggling. *Agafya,* he thought. He could see her face in his mind's eye and imagined that he could hear her gentle voice pleading with him to stay with her. He should have. He should have seen the truth then and left with her and never come back here again. He should...

The Blackfletch family tree wasn't too far away. Others followed Lyell as he was taken to it, and he felt his stomach tingling at the sight of it. He made one last attempt to pull free, but he didn't have the strength. Despair and poisoned air had left him weak.

One of the elves holding him ripped his shirt off and tossed it aside, and they slammed him into the tree, face-first.

'No,' one of them said. 'Turn him around.'

They pulled him back, turned him on the spot and shoved him back against the tree, facing them now. 'Don't,' he told them. 'Don't do this. I'm one of you, I—'

No one answered. While two elves held him still, others came over to the tree and put their hands against its trunk. He felt the faint tingle of their power moving through the wood. A deep groaning sound came from within it, and the bark began to move against his back. A great split appeared above his head and spread down to the roots, and then there was nothing behind him at all but a hole. They shoved him into it and held him there. Then the wood began to flow again. The hole began to close. Wooden bindings wrapped themselves around his arms and legs, his neck and his chest, lifting him off the ground. Lyell gasped; he could scarcely breathe. The tendrils were crushing his neck, his chest, pulling him into the heart of the tree. The split began to seal shut, from the ground up, pressing in against his chest. Soon it would cover his head. Lyell lifted his chin, trying to save himself, but the wood came up beneath it, splinters stabbing into his flesh. Thin strands of bark spread over his face.

Then it stopped. Lyell hung there, bound to the tree, only his face still visible, unable to move. He tried to speak, but there was no air in his lungs. His eyes turned, wide and bulging with pain and terror, and he looked down at them. Some of them seemed uncertain. Kiya seemed about to speak. But then one of the two who had put him into the hole spoke up.

'Leave him,' he said. 'Let him die there slowly. The tree will take him soon enough.'

Lyell tried to move, but he couldn't. He was utterly immobile. And he could feel the tree around him, slowly pulling the life force out of his body. Turning it to wood, bit by bit.

With a terrible effort, he managed to speak, his voice a rattling rasp. '*Kill... me...*'

Kiya averted her eyes.

'Come,' Eala said in a low voice. 'Don't pity him. Leave him here.'

They left, some glancing back at him with what might have been guilt, and Lyell had no more strength left to say anything. He knew that even if he did, it would go unheard. He let his eyelids droop and felt himself begin to die. Soon enough, it would be over.

Agafya, he thought. *Agafya...*

9

THE KINDNESS OF ELVES

Vender lay flat along Tail's back, held in place by a loop of string around her chest, her arms wrapped around his neck. The wind blew all around her, but she wasn't afraid of losing her hat now, and nor did her eyes sting. The dragonfly wing covered her eyes, and she had attached a strap that went under her chin to keep the wind sprites from stealing her hat again. It was working very well—they wouldn't have it now!

Vender wasn't scared of flying anymore. In fact, she was coming to love it. She looked down from Tail's back, her hair rippling in the wind, and saw everything. The long silver snake of the river, the green fields, the little brown boxes that were human houses. And by now she could see the trees ahead and knew that Silverwood was close.

They had left Vaporcitta the day after Lyell had, though the humans had asked Vender to stay. She had promised to come back again soon, once she had visited the elves. Along the way she and Tail had stopped to visit Como. Figaro and his friends were there, and they had all been thrilled to see Vender —they had asked her to stay awhile too. She had told them she would come back, too. And Figaro had said that Lyell had been there not so long ago. But when Vender told them where she was going, they had been anxious.

'You can't go into Silverwood without the elves' permission,' Figaro told her. 'Anyone who trespasses in their forest is never seen again.'

That gave Vender some pause, but she had a plan now. They wouldn't try to get into the forest. Instead, they would fly over it and find an elf. Then she could call down to them and ask if she could come in, and she wouldn't have trespassed because she wouldn't be *in* the forest, she'd be above it. That should make it all right. And anyway, she wasn't afraid of the elves. Lyell was kind and friendly; the others should be too.

Now she could see the forest, and it was beautiful. The trees were different from any of the others she had seen in Bluedell, with silvery bark and leaves. They heaved and sighed in the wind. Tail soared over them, and then started to fly lower, but Vender tugged on his crest to tell him not to, and he flew up again and started to glide, just above the treetops. A cowbird flew up at him, shrieking a warning, but the salamander blew a stream of fire that scorched the bird's wings, and it fled. Vender laughed at the sight.

Tail knew what to do. He kept going as the ground beneath the forest grew steeper, and as the trees passed by below them, Vender saw something that made her mouth drop open. A tree! A giant tree! It was bigger than any tree she had ever seen before, as tall as one of the big chimneys in Vaporcitta, its branches wide enough to cover a lake. But though the trees beyond the clearing were healthy, this tree had no leaves at all. Tail flew between the bare twigs, and Vender reached out to touch them as they passed. They did not bend and whip back, but snapped when she grabbed them—they were dead and brittle.

Tail suddenly flew lower and landed on one of the outer branches. Vender quickly pulled herself out of the string harness. In a moment she had seen them, though they looked tiny from up here. Tall, graceful figures, standing in the clearing below. They hadn't seen her, but she knew what they must be. Elves!

'*Elves!*' she hissed to Tail. '*There, elves!*'

Tail knew the plan. He jumped down to a lower branch, gripping it with his serrated claws. Then he went to another until they were low enough to see the elves clearly.

'Hello!' Vender called down to them.

Two of them looked up sharply, and one of them said something in a language Vender didn't know, but he sounded surprised.

'Hello!' she called again. 'Can I come into your forest?'

The elves were all staring at her now. Then they started to talk to each other in low, rapid voices.

'My name's Vender,' she told them. 'I was looking for my friend Lyell Blackfletch. He's from here.'

Sudden silence fell. The elves exchanged glances.

Then one of them waved to her. 'Come down here,' she said.

Vender grinned. '*Down!*' she said to Tail. '*Go to ground!*'

Tail flitted down from the tree and landed on one of its big arching roots. Vender climbed off his back and pushed the dragonfly wing up away from her eyes.

'Hello,' she said again, very excited now. She looked quickly at the little group of elves in front of her, but none of them were Lyell. Still, they had his wood-coloured skin and golden eyes, his pointed ears. Some of them were shorter than him, but they were still bigger than any human. They were looking at Vender in the same distant, veiled way Lyell had.

'Welcome,' one of them said after a pause. This was a man whose braided hair was decorated with beads. 'What brings you to Silverwood, gnome?'

'My name's Vender,' she repeated. 'And this is Tail. Lyell Blackfletch is my friend. I came here to see him. Is he here?'

The elf looked briefly at his fellows. 'How do you know Lyell?'

'I met him in Vaporcitta, when I brought the cure to the Chancellor,' Vender explained. 'He was very nice to me. He helped Tail get free as well. But then he had to go home.'

More silence. The elves were still staring at her. One or two of them looked at the one who had spoken, as if waiting for him to say something.

'So you are the one who brought the cure to the humans?' he said eventually.

'I did,' Vender said proudly. 'Fiorella made it, but she died so I took it to the city for her.'

Quite suddenly, the elf smiled a warm, friendly smile. 'Then you are welcome here,' he said. 'The hero who saved our friends the humans from the plague will always be welcome here, and I would consider it an honour. My name is Lord Brinu Skytree, the head of the Skytree family and ruler of the elves.' He bowed. 'In the name of the holy Skytree, welcome to Silverwood.'

Vender smiled back. 'Thank you! Will you show me the forest? Is Lyell here?'

Brinu shook his head. 'I am sorry, but Lyell had to leave.'

'Oh,' said Vender. 'Where did he go?'

'I sent him to visit Fivrath,' said Brinu. 'An ambassador's work is never done.'

'I was going to go there,' said Vender. 'Maybe I can find him.'

'Of course,' Brinu said kindly. 'I am sure he would be pleased to see you. But for now, will you stay with us for a while? You can see the forest, and eat with us, and hear some of our songs.'

'Yes, please!' Vender said with great enthusiasm. She was proud of herself too. She had found the elves, and they were friendly, just as she had thought they would be. Now she could go to another feast and learn more about the elves.

It was just too bad that Lyell wasn't there.

That evening, the elves gathered together in the clearing in front of the Skytree. There weren't as many as Vender had thought there would be. She wasn't very good at counting, but she thought there were about a hundred here. She watched with interest while they dug a pit in the ground and built a big bonfire in it. Others brought food: fruit and vegetables, deer carcasses, eggs, and herbs. They set to work cooking everything, and Vender sat with Tail on their root and talked to another elf who said her name was Kiya Deertrack.

'Where are your farms?' Vender asked her.

'We never farm,' said Kiya. 'That is for humans. It is not the elvish way.'

'Why not? Where do you get food?'

'Farming means the death of trees,' said Kiya. 'We gather what we need from the forest. But our true strength comes from the trees themselves.'

'Oh,' said Vender, fascinated. 'Is it true you can make them grow with magic?'

Kiya did not smile. 'We can commune with them, yes.'

'Lyell had a magic plant with him in Vaporcitta,' said Vender. 'I saw it—there were patterns on its leaves.' She paused. 'Is Lyell all right? I thought he was very sad. Do you know why he's sad, Kiya?'

The elf woman avoided her eye. 'Lyell is the last of his family,' she said. 'The Blackfletches all died long ago. That was why he chose to be the one to leave Silverwood.'

Vender sighed. 'Oh, poor Lyell. No wonder he's sad. I wish he was still here. I wanted him to show me the forest. Will *you* show it to me instead?'

Kiya looked up quickly. 'Yes, I will,' she said. 'I can show you something now, if you want.'

'All right.' Vender climbed onto Tail's back, and the salamander stood up, ready to go. Kiya beckoned to him, then turned and walked away along the edge of the clearing. Tail flew after her, jumping from branch to branch.

They left the clearing behind, but even away from the fire it wasn't dark. The air was full of fireflies, hundreds of them, their glowing bodies filling the forest with light. Tail snapped one up and quickly spat it out again. Vender took it in with awe, and thought that it was as if they were flying through the stars.

Kiya went ahead, and not too far away from the clearing they stopped at a tree that appeared different. It was taller than the others around it, with smooth brown bark and low-hanging branches. Beside it was a simple dwelling: a wooden lean-to, covered in leaves.

'Is that your home?' Vender asked.

'Yes,' said Kiya. She stopped by the tree and gently brushed its trunk with her slender fingers. 'And this is my tree. The

Deertrack family tree. My family has guarded it for generations.'

'Does Lyell have a tree too?' asked Vender.

Kiya paused. 'Yes, but you must not go looking for it. You must not go anywhere in the forest without a guide—do you understand? Silverwood is very dangerous to an outsider.'

'All right,' said Vender.

'Now,' Kiya went on. 'There is someone here you should meet.' She crouched by the lean-to and called out something in elvish. A moment later something moved inside, and Vender caught a whiff of something musky. Kiya called again, while Vender watched curiously from Tail's back, and the creature emerged.

It was about the size of a human child, but hunched and hairy, covered in shaggy black fur. Its ears were big and fringed with hair, like a donkey's ears, its paws too big for its body. Its short tail dragged on the leaf litter, and it peered at Kiya through a pair of bright yellow eyes and made a little mewling sound.

Vender started. 'That's a kobold!'

Kiya stooped to pick up the creature, which clung to her and snuffled happily at her face. Its mouth opened, showing its stubby little fangs. Kiya laughed and scratched its ears. 'This is Ferlak.'

Vender's heart was pounding. In her head, she heard Fiorella's screams. 'A kobold,' she said. 'Here?'

'Don't worry,' said Kiya. 'Ferlak is perfectly friendly. Say hello, Ferlak.'

The kobold inspected Vender, wide nostrils flaring. 'Hello, gnome,' he said in a growly little voice.

Vender started. 'He can talk?'

Ferlak grinned at her. 'Yes, we talk,' he said. 'My name Ferlak. What you name?'

'L—er, Vender.' She looked at Kiya. 'What are you doing? You could catch a plague!'

'I not sick!' Ferlak said loudly.

'Kobolds carry diseases, everyone knows that,' Vender retorted. 'And they eat people. They ate Fiorella.'

'I not eat Fiorella,' said the kobold.

'Hush,' said Kiya. She stroked Ferlak's head, and the kobold closed his eyes blissfully. 'Ferlak is not diseased. He is an orphan. I found him at the edge of the forest and took care of him. He's perfectly friendly. Kobolds are a short-lived race, and unintelligent, but they can be tamed if raised correctly.'

Vender paused. The baby kobold didn't seem dangerous. Now he was kneading at Kiya's arm with his claws, exactly like a kitten. He was even purring, or at least making a rumbly noise that might have been purring.

'Would you like to pet him?' asked Kiya. 'He won't mind.'

'All right.' Vender nudged at Tail's sides, urging him forward. The salamander pattered over to Kiya's feet, and the elf put Ferlak down beside him. Vender got off his back and looked cautiously at the kobold. Ferlak sat blinking at her for a moment, but at a gentle murmur from Kiya he came over to Vender and picked her up bodily. Vender yelped and struggled, but Ferlak only held her to his furry chest and started to pet her on the head, exactly as Kiya had done with him. His paw was big and clumsy, but his fur was warm.

'Little gnome,' he growled.

Vender hung over his arm, wincing as his paw hit her on the head. 'Put me down!'

Ferlak snuffled at her face. His nose was moist as it brushed her cheek and his breath smelled of old meat. Vender gagged. 'Stop that!'

'Put her down, Ferlak,' said Kiya.

The kobold obeyed. Vender staggered away, wiping her face. 'Your breath stinks!'

Ferlak growled at her. 'Funny gnome!'

Vender took refuge under Tail's wing, but now she found she could smile. 'You're nice,' she said. 'Not like the others.'

Ferlak grinned. 'Gnome is nice.'

'Vender,' she said. 'It was good to meet you, Ferlak. Will you come to eat with us?'

'I don't see why not,' said Kiya.

'I come!' Ferlak said eagerly, and with that he scampered off ahead of them, back toward the Skytree.

Back in the clearing the fire was burning high and bright. Moths flitted around it, and as soon as Vender was off his back, Tail flew up to chase them. The elves had waited for Vender to return before they began the meal, and as soon as she was there, sitting on her root, Brinu stood up and made a little speech just as the Chancellor had done.

'This is the first time a gnome has visited us,' he said. 'That gives Vender a special place in our history. A gnome who rides upon a salamander's back is a most unusual sight, and would be even outside our forest. But Vender is more than a curiosity; she is a hero. Because of her, the sickness the kobolds brought to the humans is no more. And now she has come all this way to visit us, despite the risk.' He gave Vender a small smile. 'For that I thank you, Vender, as do we all.'

Vender accepted their applause happily enough, and after

that they ate. The food was plain and simple, but the fruit and vegetables tasted different from any she had eaten before. There was a cleanness to them, a purity. There was only water to drink, but it was clear and sweet. While they ate, a trio of elves sang to entertain the diners. Their voices were as clear and sweet as the water. The words were in elvish, but it sounded sad and haunting to Vender. It made her think of Lyell and his sad eyes.

Later on, she came down from her root and darted between the legs of the elves with Tail chasing after her. Ferlak was there, scampering about with a deer bone clutched in one paw. Vender chased him, no longer afraid of the kobold. He was only a baby, after all, and he wanted to play. Vender tried to steal his bone, and he ran off, inviting him to chase her. She did, and Tail went with her, and the elves laughed at the sight.

Eventually, though, Ferlack grew tired and squatted down at the base of a tree by the edge of the clearing. Vender sat beside him, hugging her knees, and Tail curled up behind her and idly licked his eyeballs.

Vender leaned back against the tree, grinning broadly. 'I like you, Ferlak.'

Ferlak crunched on his bone. 'Gnome is good friend!'

She patted him cautiously on the elbow. 'I just hope you stay nice when you get bigger.'

He didn't answer that. He gnawed on his bone—and then paused. His big ears flicked and turned, tilting back to listen. His head went up, and he dropped the bone and began to sniff at the air.

Vender watched him. 'What is it?'

Ferlak got up and turned, watching the dark forest behind them, both ears fully erect. He snuffled and his tail twitched.

Vender got up and followed his gaze, but she couldn't see or hear anything. 'What is it?' she said again.

Ferlak stood still a moment longer, then suddenly bounded off into the trees.

'Hey!' Vender looked back at the elves, but none of them seemed to have noticed. She hesitated, then ran after the kobold as fast as she could go. Tail ran after her.

There were more fireflies here, but the light was still dim. Vender could see Ferlak's shaggy shape up ahead, still bounding over the ground like a rabbit. He was much faster than he appeared. She briefly thought of what Kiya had said, which was that she shouldn't be out here by herself. It was dangerous. But she couldn't let Ferlak run away. He might get hurt.

Tail caught up with her and nudged at her side, urging her to get onto his back. She took hold of his crest and was about to pull herself up—but then she heard it. The sound, drifting toward her through the trees.

It sounded like a voice, but there were no words. Only a sound. A high, strangled, terrible sound. Vender froze to the spot, her spine tingling. She had never heard anything like that before, or had she?

The cry came again, and that was when Vender knew what it was.

Someone was screaming.

Vender only stayed still a moment longer. She hauled herself onto Tail's back. 'Go,' she told him. '*Go now, go fast! Fast!*'

Tail ran, scampering over leaves and roots, still chasing after Ferlak. The screaming had stopped, but in a way the sudden silence was worse.

Then Vender saw Ferlak. He had stopped at the base of a

tree, and there beside him was a deer. A huge one, lying on her belly by the tree's trunk. It saw them and huffed softly through its nostrils.

Tail came to a stop by Ferlak. The kobold wasn't paying any attention to them. He was staring up at the tree's branches.

Vender nudged him. 'Ferlak, what is it? What did you find?'

Ferlak was whining. 'Hurt,' he said. 'Very hurt.'

'What?' said Vender. 'You—'

Then she heard it. Something else, coming from above them. A strange, thin, rattling, rasping sound. It was coming from the tree. She looked up, and now she could see something there, a strange shape in the trunk. But what could it be?

Ferlak pawed at the bark. 'Elf is hurt,' he whimpered.

Vender glanced over at the deer, which stared back sadly at her. She could still hear the rasping sound coming from the tree and realised it was the sound of painful breathing.

Quickly, she urged Tail over toward the deer. He went, and despite the deer's faint sound of complaint, he climbed up her flank and then swarmed up her neck and onto her head. And from there, Vender could make out what it was.

There was a face in the tree, an elvish face. Part of one cheek had turned to bark, and more bark went over the nose and forehead, but Vender still knew it.

'Lyell,' she breathed.

Lyell's golden eyes were dim, the lids drooping, and she could hear his strangled breaths.

'Lyell!' Vender jumped off Tail's back and ran to the end of the deer's muzzle. She reached up to touch Lyell's face. It was warm. She took hold of the strand of bark that went over his chin and wrenched at it. It peeled away from his skin, and a line of raw flesh appeared beneath it. Lyell's eyes opened wide and he screamed again.

There was blood on Vender's hands. She backed away, horrified. 'I'm sorry! I didn't mean to... Lyell...'

The elf's breathing grew even harsher. He stared at Vender, eyes bulging.

'Lyell,' she said. 'What happened to you?'

Lyell's eyes drooped again. '*Vender...*' His voice was scarcely more than a whisper.

'Yes, it's Vender. Lyell, what... what happened?'

'Punishment,' he whispered. 'You should... not... be... here.'

'But I came to see you!' said Vender. 'They said you were gone away again.'

Blood slowly trickled down Lyell's chin, where the bark had been torn away. 'Go,' he said. 'Go...'

'I can't just leave you here!' said Vender.

'No,' he whispered. 'No... can't... help. I will be... dead... soon.'

Vender heard him, and felt something she had never felt before. True fear. True horror. How could anyone...?

'Who did this?' she asked in a small voice. 'Why?'

'Brinu,' Lyell gasped. 'I was meant... the cure... told me to destroy it. I couldn't... couldn't do it. Go... Vender. They will make you sick... send you home... your people... their own plague. We...' He took in another slow, weak breath. 'We... kill...'

'What?' said Vender. 'You mean the plagues. But that was the kobolds.'

'Lies,' said Lyell. 'Elvish... lies. Go. Get away.'

Vender touched his face again. 'But there has to be something I can do. How can I save you?'

Lyell managed to look at her. 'Agafya,' he whispered.

'Agafya Ivano. A dwarf. Find her... in the blasted lands. West of here. Edge of... the forest. Find her. Tell her...'

'What? What should I tell her? Can she help you?'

'Tell her I am sorry,' said Lyell. 'Ask her... forgive me. Tell her... I love her. Promise you... do that. For me.'

'I will, I will, and I'll bring her here to save you,' said Vender.

'No,' Lyell gasped. 'No, don't. Don't. They... kill her. Leave me. I deserve... this.'

Vender ran back to Tail and got onto his back. 'I'll save you, Lyell,' she promised. 'I'll find Agafya and she'll help me.'

'No,' the elf pleaded. 'No, don't. Don't...'

'I'll come back soon,' said Vender. *'Tail, we fly! Fly west!'*

She took one last look at Lyell, who was staring at her with those sad eyes, and then Tail took off, flying up toward the forest canopy, leaving Furlak curled up at the base of the tree and the deer keeping her silent vigil.

10

THE BLASTED LANDS

There was no joy in Vender's flight out of Silverwood. Tail was tired, but she urged him on, and he flew west as fast as he could. Vender clung on, teeth gritted. She had to do this. Now, for the first time, there was something in her that gave her a true sense of urgency and panic. She had flown to Vaporcitta to save the humans, but only because Fiorella had asked her to. They weren't her people, even if she liked them. Of course, Lyell wasn't one of her people either, but...

All she could see in her mind's eye was his tortured face staring at her from his prison. He was dying in there, and his own people had done it to him.

I have to save him, she thought. She felt as if she would die herself if she left him there like that.

Eventually, with dawn beginning to glow on the horizon, Tail refused to fly any further. He landed on a large tree branch and grumpily tipped Vender off his back. She sat down beside him, legs dangling.

'*Rest now?*' she said reluctantly.

Tail curled up. '*Rest,*' he hissed, and promptly went to sleep.

Vender stretched out on her back, not even thinking to look down to find out how high they were. There were bigger things on her mind now. What had Lyell said? That the plagues came from the elves? But that couldn't be true, could it?

But he had been ordered to destroy the cure, and the cure had been stolen and then returned. Lyell had taken it and then changed his mind. He had let the humans keep it, and now he was being killed for not doing what he was meant to. And Vender... they had been going to make her sick. Give her a disease that would kill the other gnomes and her as well.

And they had seemed so kind, so friendly... How could that be? How could someone seem to be one thing but actually be something else? It made no sense. And what was the point of pretending like that? It was lying. The thought left her feeling hurt and confused.

Lyell... Lyell would understand. If she could rescue him, maybe he could teach her what it all meant.

When Tail eventually woke up, Vender shook off the light doze she had slipped into and got onto his back.

'*Tired,*' Tail complained. '*Hungry.*'

'*Rest, eat later,*' Vender told him. '*Go now—go west.*'

Reluctantly, Tail launched himself off the branch and flew on. It was midmorning now, judging by the sun, and Vender's head was pounding. Her stomach was rumbling too, but she didn't have any food with her. Tail, at least, managed to feed himself, snapping up insects on the wing.

Meanwhile, the forest had begun to thin out, and ahead she

could see a great expanse of black, barren ground. They were nearly there.

At the edge of the forest, the trees had been reduced to stumps, sticking up out of the ashy ground like charred black rotten teeth. And further west there was nothing growing at all. How had this happened?

Tail seemed to like it here, though. He landed on a stump and vigorously scratched his flank, his tongue flicking all the while. *'Ash,'* he hissed. *'Ash and charcoal.'*

Vender hadn't heard him say anything that complicated before. 'Yes, everything here is burned,' she agreed. 'Do you think it was the dwarves?' She remembered from the map that Fivrath was somewhere further west of here.

'Wait, dwarves eat charcoal, don't they?' she said to herself. 'Then if Agafya is here, she must be using the stumps for food.' It made sense, so she patted Tail on the neck and said, *'Look, look dwarf now. Find dwarf!'* She knew he must know what a dwarf looked like—he had come from Fivrath, after all.

Sure enough, Tail said, *'Find dwarf,'* and flew away along the edge of the trees.

The blasted lands seemed to go on forever, and so did the stumps. There didn't seem to be anyone here at all. How long were they going to have to search?

The day wore on, and exhaustion tugged at Vender's eyelids. She couldn't remember the last time she had had a proper night's sleep, and her hunger was only growing worse. But there was nothing here to eat.

Toward evening, hunger tearing at her insides, she began to tell Tail they should stop. She could go back into the forest on foot and see what she could find to eat.

Tail landed on a stump and fluttered his wings. He was hissing. *'Taste.'* His tongue flicked in and out. *'Taste danger.'*

Vender looked ahead, puzzled. But then something she had thought was a big grey rock suddenly moved. Vender yelped in surprise as a head lifted into view. It was bigger than Tail, long and heavy, and as it moved its jaws opened, showing rows of sharp jagged teeth.

'What is *that*?' Vender exclaimed.

The thing had seen them. Its head turned toward them, and a long forked tongue flicked out of its mouth. It was a lizard the size of a horse, Vender realised. It started to lumber toward them, its long claws sinking into the ash. Its back was hunched, covered in thick grey scales, and a long heavy tail waved behind it. There were spikes on its head, and more on its tail, and its little eyes were fixed on them.

Tail didn't wait to be asked. He flew up off the stump and out of reach, while Vender watched the giant creature in awe. It looked up at them and opened its mouth, a growl rumbling in its chest. Vender was very, very glad they were out of its reach —it could have eaten them both in one mouthful.

'*Tail*,' she said. '*Fly—*'

Before she could finish, a shout came from the shelter of the trees, speaking a language she had never heard before. '*Nyet! Idi syuda, Esfir!*'

The lizard turned around at once and then stomped away toward the source of the voice. Vender saw the figure emerge into the open. It was about the size of a human, but much wider, with skin the colour of the burned wood all about. The hair, though, was a startling shade of yellow.

A dwarf!

The dwarf went over to the lizard and started to pat it on the muzzle, murmuring to it. It hissed at her and closed its eyes.

Vender pulled urgently on Tail's crest. '*Fly! Fly down! Fly to branch!*'

With some coaxing, Tail came in to land on a branch above the dwarf's head. From there, Vender shouted. 'Hello, dwarf!'

The dwarf turned around, and exclaimed something in a language Vender didn't know.

'Hello,' Vender said again. 'I'm Vender. Are you Agafya Ivano?'

'I am,' said the dwarf, breaking into the human language, which she spoke with a thick accent. She looked bewildered. 'A gnome riding a salamander? Where did you come from?'

Vender's heart leaped. 'I've come from Silverwood,' she said in a rush. 'Lyell sent me to find you.'

Agafya stiffened at once, her hand on her pet's head. 'Lyell? Lyell Blackfletch?'

'Yes, he needs your help,' said Vender. 'He's...' She paused and winced. 'It's the other elves. They put him into a tree.'

Agafya's eyes widened. 'They... the ritual punishment...'

'Yes, and it's *killing* him,' Vender said desperately. 'I could hear him screaming. And he said—'

The dwarf's broad chest began to heave. 'No. Oh, no.'

'He said to tell you he was sorry. He said he wanted you to forgive him. And he said he loves you.'

Agafya shuddered. 'Not him. Not my Lyell.'

'We have to rescue him!' said Vender. 'We have to take him out of there, before...'

Agafya grabbed hold of one of the lizard's head spikes. 'Yes,' she said. 'Yes, we must. Let me gather my things. We must be going at once.' She said something to the lizard, which followed her up along the treeline. Vender and Tail followed.

Not far away, Agafya had set up a camp for herself. There wasn't much in it—only a rough shelter made from sticks and a blanket. An axe stuck out of a stump beside it. Agafya went into the shelter and dragged some items out—a metal breastplate and greaves, a helmet, and a leather saddle and harness. She pulled on the armour, then strapped the saddle and harness onto the lizard.

'What is that?' asked Vender, unable to stop herself.

'A saurian,' Agafya said shortly. She wrenched the axe out of the stump and put it into her belt, then climbed onto the beast's back and took the reins. The saurian growled, and Agafya looked sharply at Vender. 'Show us the way.'

Vender pointed Tail east, and the salamander flew away, low through the trees. There were some strange flowers growing at the edge of the forest—yellow, with bulging green lumps inside them. Vender checked to see if Agafya was still following, but the dwarf had suddenly pulled her mount to a halt. Tail landed on a branch.

'What is it—' Vender started to say, but the dwarf cut her off.

'Move,' she said harshly. 'Go to safe distance.'

Tail quickly flitted on deeper into the forest, and not a moment too soon. Agafya raised both her hands and fire streamed out of her palms. It hit the flowers, which started to wither. Then they exploded. Bright green dust puffed into the air and immediately turned to ashes. Agafya kept going, sending her fire around both sides of the saurian's head until the undergrowth in their path had been reduced to nothing but scorched ground.

'Why did you do that?' Vender exclaimed.

The fire stopped and Agafya took the reins and urged the saurian on. 'Poison blooms,' she said shortly. 'A defence to stop intruders.' She kicked the saurian in the sides, and the beast hissed and charged away into the forest. Tail kicked away from his branch and flew ahead.

They rode on through the night, and Agafya refused to stop. She leaned forward in the saddle, while the saurian charged through the trees with astonishing speed. Tail and Vender flew ahead to scout the way, then returned—the saurian wasn't hard to find. It crashed through the trees and bushes like a charging bull, its tail spikes leaving deep gashes in the tree trunks as it passed. When the ground grew rocky and steep, it bounded over the obstacles in its way with no trouble at all.

Tail, on the other hand, had had enough. He landed on the creature's back, behind Agafya, and stayed there. Vender was happy to let him. She lay back against his side and promptly went to sleep, too exhausted to even notice the constant lurching and the thud of claws.

When she woke up, it was to find that the saurian had finally stopped moving. It was lying down now, head on its claws, fast asleep. Daylight had come, and Agafya was nearby, sitting by a fire.

Vender sat up blearily. Tail was still asleep. 'Hello, Agafya.'

The dwarf put her hand into the fire, not seeming to feel it at all, and pulled out a lump of burning coal. 'Vender, good morning.'

Vender rubbed her eyes. 'How far did we go?'

'A long way.' Agafya stared at the coal through her strange blue and silver eyes, then sighed and bit into it.

'I don't know how long it will take us to get to Lyell,' said Vender. 'I could fly there quickly, but—'

'We must be going there at night,' Agafya interrupted. 'To save him while the others are sleeping. So we travel at night and sleep in the day. You must go ahead, to make sure no one sees us.'

'I will,' said Vender.

Agafya took another coal from the fire. 'Where did you come from, Vender?' she asked. 'Why were you in Silverwood?'

Vender explained.

Agafya seemed puzzled. 'What a strange gnome you are.'

'Everybody says that,' Vender complained. 'I'm not just a gnome, I'm Vender. I don't think being a gnome is that important, or an elf, or a human either.'

'Perhaps not,' Agafya said with a smile.

'But what about you?' said Vender. 'How do you know Lyell? Was it when he was in Fivrath?'

The dwarf crunched on her coal, and her eyes grew brighter. 'Yes, he was ambassador there for years. All through the plague. I was in Silverwood before, when the elves invited me to visit with them. Lyell came back with me. But then we were attacked by kobolds, on the blasted plain. We escaped, but I was sick when we came to Fivrath. Others caught the sickness and died... My family, all gone. All that was left to me was Lyell.'

'You love him,' said Vender.

'I do,' said Agafya. 'More than life. And he promised we could be together one day. But then he told me I must leave Fivrath and hide myself away, for my safety.'

'Why?'

'Because... a message was given to him from Silverwood, telling him he must kill me. He could not say why, but if they knew he let me live, he would be... given to the tree. I promised I would wait for him, and I have. But now...'

'Now he needs us to save him,' said Vender. 'Do you know how? Can you take him out of the tree?'

'I don't know,' said Agafya. 'But I must try. I must.' And her eyes grew brighter than ever.

11

UPROOTED

Lyell couldn't see much anymore. The bark had grown over his left eyelid, and it was so stiff he couldn't make it open all the way. But he could still see out of the other eye, even if he couldn't turn his head, and he could hear—the lower parts of his ears were still exposed.

He couldn't feel much of his body anymore, and that was a blessing in a way. All the sensation had left his arms and legs. They were one with the tree, and the numbness was spreading over his chest. He could feel his heart beating, and he could breathe, but soon enough his heart and lungs would turn to wood, and then he would die. The bark would cover the rest of his face, and then there would be nothing left of him at all, only a bulge in the trunk to show that Lyell Blackfletch had ever existed.

Here, there was only the pain left to let him know he was still alive.

He managed to move his head a fraction. Leaf was still there, patiently waiting for him. He whispered to her to go, but she stayed. She would wait here until he was dead. At least he wasn't alone here, not quite.

The baby kobold was still there, too. He couldn't see it, but he could hear it snuffling somewhere.

He looked out at the trees in front of him and dragged in another agonising breath. Dawn had come. How much longer would he last? How many more dawns before the sight was gone from his eyes?

Agafya, he thought.

Movement caught his eye. Kiya.

The other elf paused at the sight of him, then looked away and beckoned at something on the ground. There was a rustling of leaf litter, and the baby kobold came into view, padding over to his guardian. Kiya scooped him up, still looking away from Lyell.

Lyell breathed in again. 'Kiya,' he whispered.

She did not reply.

'Kiya,' he said again. 'Please... look... at me.'

She hesitated.

'Kiya.' His voice gurgled in his crushed chest. 'I am... sorry.'

Kiya stared at the ground. 'How could you do this to us, Lyell?' she said. 'You were... you were the bravest of us, the strongest. We put all our faith in you. *I* put my faith in you. You could have saved us—you could have saved the Skytree. How could you betray us like this?'

Lyell's bark-covered eyelid drooped. 'Because I... c...cared... about... them.'

'But you should have cared for us more,' said Kiya.

Lyell said nothing.

'Your pet gnome was here,' Kiya added. 'The one you were meant to kill. She has her punishment now. The infection is on her. Soon those filthy little creatures will be gone from our land.'

No, they won't, Lyell thought with a flare of weak satisfaction. *I warned her.*

'Our quest will be completed,' Kiya told him. 'Soon enough. Hylah will be cleansed. The forest will grow back, the Skytree will flourish. You know that, don't you? Your betrayal will change nothing. Maybe that will comfort you in your last hours.'

Finally, Lyell managed to speak. 'You... are fools.'

Kiya threw a last look at him and walked away. The baby kobold looked back at Lyell over her shoulder and whimpered softly.

Then Lyell was alone again, other than the silent presence of Leaf. He watched in silence as the day passed by, the shadows shifting on the forest floor by his tree. At least, he thought, his final resting place would be a fitting one. If he had died before, they would have merged his body with this tree, the Blackfletch tree, where his ancestors and all family rested; flesh and bone now living wood. No, this was the right place for him, and perhaps a part of his soul would live on as the tree grew. And this was a beautiful place. He had missed it so much.

But still... he did not want to die.

Agafya.

He thought of Vender too. She was such a strange little thing. An adult by the years of her kind, and yet she was so much like a child. Gnomes were simple creatures, their outlook on the world a childish one. But they were incurious, with no interest in anything beyond their own simple lives. Vender was different. Other gnomes looked inward, but she looked out. She had qualities they didn't: imagination, thoughtfulness, a lust for adventure. But she was still so naïve. How long could she possibly survive out there? The world was a harsher place than she could ever know.

Still, he had given her a chance to live, and he could only hope that she would find Agafya and give her his last message... and that Agafya would have the sense not to try to save him, even if he would have given anything to see her face one last time.

He dozed, woke, and dozed again. Another day came and went. He could feel the skin over the left side of his face gradually growing stiffer. The bark was spreading. Now he couldn't blink with the eye on that side at all. All that was left to him was a slit.

Bit by bit, his lips began to stiffen too. Soon enough he would be unable to talk. His left ear sank into the tree trunk, lost. His hearing was fading.

Nobody else came to see him. Nobody wanted to. Animals came and went, and Leaf wandered away to browse before returning to his side.

Another day. Breathing was growing harder and harder. His heartbeat slowed. He could feel the sap of the tree flowing through his veins, replacing his blood.

One more night, he thought. *One more night and one more day.*

At least there wasn't much pain anymore.

That last night came soon enough—time seemed to pass more quickly now. Lyell watched the fireflies through his remaining eye. He could hear their faint buzzing.

But then he heard something else. A rustling sound. Footsteps. Someone was coming.

Lyell wrenched his eyelid back and stared out at the trees.

There was light... faint light, coming closer. He struggled to think. What could that be? Who?

Something came shooting out of the trees—something long and dark. It landed on the startled Leaf's head, and an instant later Lyell heard the voice, small and quick, and full of fear.

'Lyell! Lyell!'

His heart sank. Vender. Vender had come back. *Go,* he tried to say, but the word wouldn't come.

Vender touched his bark-covered cheek. 'She's coming,' she said. 'Agafya's coming. She's here!'

The short, dark figure rode toward him on the back of her saurian, her armour gleaming in the light of the torch she carried in one hand. Her eyes were wide, fixed on his face, and at the sight of her a hideous pain shot through his heart. He gasped.

Agafya reined in her mount, leaped down, and ran toward him. 'Lyell! Oh, Lyell.'

Lyell whispered her name.

She put her arms around the tree, embracing it and him, and kissed his cheek. 'Lyell, my Lyell, my dear one.'

It hurt to move his lips, but Lyell forced himself to. '*Go...*'

'No, my love,' Agafya said, not letting him go. 'Never. I must... I must save you. Tell me what to do.'

Lyell's eye closed. 'I am... one... with the wood,' he said. 'While the tree... lives... it...' His lips cracked and began to bleed, and the last of his breath left him. He fell silent, unable to say anymore.

A moment later he heard Vender's shout. 'Burn it!' she said. 'Burn him out of there, Agafya!'

Agafya let go of the tree. 'I could burn the wood away from him.'

Lyell's eye opened. *No,* he thought. *No!*

'Do it,' Vender was saying. 'Hurry!'

Agafya took a step back. She shoved Leaf away, and the deer retreated, Vender still standing on her head. The saurian hissed at her.

The dwarf raised her hands and flames appeared around them. Lyell's eye widened. *No!* , but his bleeding lips would not move. *No, don't! STOP!*

Lyell's eye widened. *No!* he tried to say, but his bleeding lips would not move. *No, don't! STOP!*

'Don't be afraid, my love,' she said. 'I can do this.'

She sent her flames at the tree. The bark blackened, and then the wood beneath began to turn to charcoal. And Lyell felt it. He felt the sap boiling, the living wood of the tree screaming as it split in the heat. He felt the tree's pain and he began to scream, a wordless, strangled scream.

But Agafya did not stop. Eyes narrow beneath her helmet, she moved her flames up and down the trunk, the length of Lyell's body, slowly eating away at the wood. Lyell's sap-infused blood began to boil, his bark skin bubbled and flaked away, his wooden flesh crumbled, and as the pain consumed him along with his prison, he began to feel something else. His limbs. He could feel them. The sensation was coming back into his arms and legs.

Terrified, he tried to move, and his head broke away. The tree screamed around him, its pain was his pain. The wood fell from it in chunks. Convulsing now, wreathed in flame, Lyell struggled with all his might. One arm ripped free, and then the other, and as the tree's trunk broke in half, he fell forward onto the dirt, burned and bleeding and gasping for breath. Behind him, the tree came crashing down. Dead.

Lyell lay face-down, his whole body wracked with pain, only vaguely aware of the voices of the others. But then Agafya was there. Her hot hands took him by the shoulder and turned him over, and then she was holding onto him, hugging him to her. 'Lyell, Lyell...'

He began to cough, and it shook his whole body. Pain cracked through his spine, and he groaned. His lips were still bleeding, still stiff with bark. 'Agafya...' He winced as more blood wet his chin.

From somewhere nearby, Vender shouted. 'Someone's coming!'

Agafya quickly got to her feet, lifting Lyell with her. She was shorter than him, but powerfully muscled, and she pulled him away from the tree stump without much trouble, toward the waiting Leaf. Vender was there, with Tail, wearing a dumbfounded expression.

Vender was there, with Tail, wearing a dumbfounded expression. 'He's covered in wood.'

Lyell looked down at himself through blurry eyes. His pants were ruined, and his legs and exposed chest were covered in splinters and long twisted strands of green timber, as if he had fur or bristles like a hedgehog. Some of it was blackened, some stained with blood. A strangled laugh escaped him at the sight.

Leaf nudged at him, urging him to get onto her back. Agafya touched his right cheek, the one still untouched by bark.

'Can you stand? Can you ride?'

Lyell tried to stand up. His legs were weak and aching, and sharp pains spiked through the soles of his feet as the splinters there went in deeper. But he felt... strong. Much stronger than he had thought he would be. He threw an arm around Leaf's neck, ignoring the pain, and Agafya helped him onto the deer's back. Leaf stood up, even as a pair of figures came hurrying toward them from the direction of the Skytree. Two elvish women, Kiya and Eala, stopped in shock at the sight of him.

'Lyell!' Eala exclaimed.

Agafya growled and pulled out her axe. A moment later, its blades burst into flame and began to glow red-hot.

Eala pulled her bow down off her back and notched an arrow. 'Stay back, dwarf.'

At that moment, seeing its mistress threatened, the saurian suddenly reared up out of the gloom. It roared and lumbered forward, fangs bared. Eala loosed her arrow at it, but it bounced off the creature's scales, and the saurian charged.

'Stop!' Lyell rasped. 'Agafya, we must go!'

Agafya shouted a dwarvish command at the saurian, and it skidded to a halt and ran back to her. She vaulted onto its back and hurled fire at the two elves. Kiya leaped out of the way. Tail came swooping out of nowhere and spat a fireball at Eala.

Lyell held onto Leaf's neck and urged the deer away. She turned north and galloped away into the wood, and he heard the crashing commotion behind him as the saurian followed.

The elf's head was spinning. He felt too dazed even to care about the wood embedded in his backside and legs, tearing at his skin with every movement. He was free. He was alive. But the Blackfletch family tree was dead. The tree of his ancestors was dead, and he was an outcast.

But, he thought, *I am not alone.*

Leaf knew which way to go. She fled from the clearing and the fallen tree, dodging anything in her path. The light from Agafya's burning axe helped to show the way ahead, though her saurian was slower. The creature's scent might even have encouraged the deer to run faster.

Lyell held on, feeling the wood embedded in his body—it was in his fingers and the palms of his hands. The bark was still on his face, and he ached all over. But something else felt different—something deep inside, though he couldn't tell what it was.

The forest gradually began to grow thicker until Leaf couldn't pass through it anymore. Now she turned east, not slowing her pace at all, Agafya still on her heels. Lyell didn't know where Vender was—he hoped she was still with them.

The sky was lightening now—dawn was coming. Leaf splashed through a stream and bounded up the side of the rocky outcrop on the far side. At its top was a tree—huge, though not as huge as the Skytree, and long dead.

Lyell slid off her back and gasped when he hit the ground. He pulled himself up with a groan, patted Leaf on the nose, and limped over to the dead tree. Its trunk was hollow, and he sat down inside it and checked himself. The wood hanging out of him looked worse than ever.

Agafya came to join him, her face ashen. 'My Lyell, how are you?'

Lyell smiled wanly at her, ignoring the pain in his cracked lips. 'You saved my life.'

Agafya smiled back. '*We* saved your life,' she said. And there was Vender, perched on Tail's back, flying down from the saurian's head to join them.

'Vender,' Lyell said hoarsely. 'There you are.'

The gnome's small, pale face was full of concern. 'Are you all right, Lyell?'

Lyell inspected his splinter-filled arm. He hesitated, then

took hold of one of the larger pieces of wood and tugged at it. It slid out of his flesh and a small trickle of liquid followed.

It was not blood.

Lyell dabbed at it and held his fingers up to his face. It was close to blood, but the colour was wrong. There was a greenish tint to it now, and it smelled of freshly cut timber.

'Sap,' he said blankly. 'There is sap...'

Agafya touched him carefully. 'What is it, my love?'

Lyell looked up at her. 'There is... sap in my blood.'

'Oh!' said Vender. 'Will that hurt you?'

'I don't know.' Lyell pulled out another shard of wood, and then another, slowly plucking them out of his arm. The skin underneath was still skin, and the flesh was still flesh and had lost none of its suppleness. But he knew something inside had changed. The tree was still in him.

'I will be awhile in healing,' he said at last. 'But I think I will recover.'

'You will!' Vender said cheerfully.

Agafya glanced at the gnome and smiled. 'Will we be safe here, Lyell?'

'For now,' he said. 'They will come looking for us, but this is a place my people dislike.'

'Why?' asked Vender.

'This tree here... this was the tree of the Blueleaf family. But they are all dead now, and their tree has died as well. We think of this as a cursed place. But I used to come here... after my family died. It was a reminder to me of what we had lost. What we were losing.'

After a moment's hesitation, Agafya squeezed into the hollow and sat down beside him. 'What do you mean, my love?'

Lyell pulled out a handful of splinters and winced. 'The

forest is dying,' he said. 'The trees are dying. The Skytree... it was dying when I left, but now it is dead. My people are in decline and have been for a long time.'

'It seems as if every race is dying,' said Agafya. 'Mine, the humans, the elves...'

'I know,' said Lyell. He rubbed his face, feeling the bark covering it. Most of his hair had been torn away. 'Agafya, I... when I came to Fivrath with you, I...'

'What is it?' she asked.

Lyell avoided her eye. 'You should not have saved me. After what I did, I should have been left to die.'

'No, Lyell. I will not be hearing that. Tell me the truth.' Her gaze was penetrating.

'Yes, you deserve to know it. Then here it is.' Lyell took a deep breath. 'The kobold attack was a ruse. My people—we steal infant kobolds and train them to work for us. They lead their kind to attack when and where we order them to. They attacked you and I on our way to Fivrath, so you would believe that when you became sick, it was because of them. But it was not. The disease was planted on you long before then, while you were still in Silverwood. My task was to take you back to Fivrath, where you could infect your entire race, then make certain that they never found a cure. I was there for one reason: to oversee the extinction of the dwarven race.'

Agafya said nothing. She was staring at him, wide-eyed.

'Afterward,' Lyell went on, 'I was expected to assassinate you, in case you came to suspect the truth. I nearly did that day, when you asked me to take you away. But... I could not bring myself to do it. I had seen so much suffering, and I had come to love you... I should have stopped it there, but I still believed it was necessary.'

Vender stood nearby with her salamander, her expression horrified. '*Why* was it necessary?'

'Because I believed the Skytree would come back to life if Hylah was... cleansed,' said Lyell. 'If the other races were driven away. We are a very old people, and when the world around us changed we could not understand it, and we blamed the coming of humans and dwarves. To us, it was a threat to our way of life. A threat to the forest, and the Skytree, and all of us. I... I was not... the first. There were others before me. But I was the first to weaken. I was so certain, I left here with nothing in my heart but anger and resolve, I cared for nothing but my own people. But you changed me, Agafya. After I came to know you, I could not... I could not harden my heart against what I was seeing, what I was allowing. And then when I was sent to the humans, and it all began again, I could not bear it.'

Agafya said nothing. She was still staring at him in shock and disbelief.

Lyell wanted to touch her, but did not. 'Then the cure came,' he said. 'Vender brought it. My orders were to destroy the cure and kill the one who brought it. That was why I let you into my room, Vender. I meant to kill you that day. But I talked to you instead, and you were... I saw you were an innocent. Killing you would have been no different to killing a baby in the cradle. I could not do it. So I left the city and came back here, to confront Lord Brinu. I told him that what we were doing was wrong, it was evil. They would not listen. They called me traitor and gave me to the tree.'

Lyell had said all he had to say, and now he shuddered into silence and sat staring at his mutilated body.

'That's so terrible,' said Vender. 'You were trying to do what was right and they did that to you.'

Lyell looked quickly at her. 'You are infected now,' he said. 'I think you must be. They made you a carrier, like Agafya.'

Vender's eyes widened. 'What's going to happen to me?'

'You will fall sick,' Lyell told her. 'It will happen within a week. But you will recover. If you stay away from other gnomes until then, all will be well. Otherwise, they will be infected and die.'

Vender seemed relieved. 'Well, I won't go back to my old home,' she said. 'I'm staying with you and Agafya.'

Agafya still said nothing. Lyell waited wretchedly, knowing there was nothing he could say to undo his confession.

The dwarf stood up with a sudden jerky motion. She was staring at him, her blue and silver eyes full of horror. 'You,' she whispered. 'You...'

Lyell did not move. 'I am... sorry, Agafya. So sorry. I should have told you the truth before. I was a coward.'

Agafya's hand went to her axe, as if she were about to draw it, but she let go of it and hit Lyell across the face—a burning-hot, powerful slap that slammed his head back against the dead tree.

Vender yelped. 'Stop that! Don't—'

Pain crackled through Lyell's skull. He heaved himself up with a groan. 'Agafya.'

She stood over him, breathing hard through her nostrils, and then slapped him a second time. Red lights exploded in front of his eyes and he reeled backward, but made no effort to defend himself.

'Stop it!' Vender yelled again. Incredibly, she rushed over to Agafya and grabbed her by the leg, making a futile attempt to pull her away. 'You're hurting him!'

Agafya paused, her hand still raised, then stooped and

picked the gnome up bodily. 'You would defend him?' she said harshly. 'After what he has done?'

Vender gasped in the dwarf's powerful grip. 'But he's sorry! He tried to make it better. He loves you.'

Lyell struggled to his feet. 'Vender, stop. Please stop.'

Agafya snarled. She thrust Vender into Lyell's hands and then turned away.

Lyell didn't try to go after her. 'Agafya, I am sorry,' he said yet again. 'You should... you should have left me to die.'

'Yes,' she said abruptly. 'I should have.'

The saurian was waiting, hissing to itself. Agafya hauled herself onto the beast's back and urged it away. The saurian charged away into the trees, spiked tail leaving deep gashes in the trunks, great clawed feet thudding on the leaf litter.

'Come back!' Vender shouted. 'Agafya, come back! Where are you going?'

Agafya didn't reply. The saurian sped up and in moments it was gone.

'We have to go after her! Lyell, what are you doing? She might get into trouble.'

Lyell stared fixedly at the trees where Agafya had been. He felt an agonising wrenching at his heart, and it was far more painful than that of his ravaged body. 'I cannot go with her,' he said in a low voice. His face was stinging—the bark had split under Agafya's hand, and sap-filled blood wet his cheek.

'Why not?' Vender demanded. 'You love each other, don't you? Why can't she just forgive you?'

Lyell put her down beside Tail. 'What I have done... cannot be forgiven,' he said.

'But why not?' said Vender. She climbed onto Tail's back.

Lyell slumped down on his seat and continued to pull the shards of wood out of himself, though he moved stiffly and unnaturally now, like one of the humans' machines. 'Enough, Vender,' he said, just as stiffly. 'That's enough.'

The gnome stopped talking, but she still looked confused and unhappy. She petted Tail's head.

Lyell pulled one of the bigger pieces of wood out of his left arm and winced as the hole it left behind began to bleed freely. He could see the muscle under his skin, all exposed, and it was... green. The pale green of tree sap wove in among the red of elvish flesh, as if...

I am one with the tree, he thought dully. *It is in me.*

Vender was watching, though she kept glancing over her shoulder as if she expected to see Agafya returning. 'You can do magic with plants, can't you?' she said abruptly. 'Can you do magic with that wood stuck in you?'

Lyell paused, one hand covering the bleeding wound. 'I... perhaps...'

'Can you?' said Vender.

Lyell said nothing. After a moment's thought, he closed his eyes and felt for it, sensing the energy around him. There was still the faintest trace of it in the tree at his back. Even dead wood held some magic. But there was another source of natural power much closer, and it was... different. The power of an ancestral tree, thrumming with life—a tree he had sensed many times before. The Blackfletch tree. But now that energy was coming from inside his own body.

A strange ecstasy pulsed through his head. Acting on instinct, he let his natural gift join with the energy he could sense, communing with the tree. In an instant, the two of them locked together, elf and tree, and at once a great blast of pain struck him, from the chest outward. Pain, and strength.

Lyell's eyes snapped open and he breathed in sharply. All over his skin, the wood stuck in him began to move. The bark on his face flowed outward, and even as he looked down at himself he saw it happen. The shards of living wood pulled inward, sucked through his skin and into his body, where it disappeared. The skin sealed over without a trace of scarring, but it had changed. Faint patterns emerged on his arms and his bare chest, and he knew them at once. He was covered in the rippling marks of wood grain.

The pain was gone.

Lyell touched his face. The bark was gone too, though he could feel the thick seam of a scar on his chin where Vender had torn a strip of it away. He heaved a sigh.

Vender was watching him with an expression of wonder. 'You did it! You're healed!'

Lyell rubbed his forehead. 'Yes. I did not stop to think if... But I should be fine now. I feel much stronger.'

'What are we going to do now, then?' asked Vender. 'Are we going to find Agafya?'

'No,' he said, a pang at his heart. 'I must go; I am an exile now.' He stood up. 'I will find a place to hide, but nowhere will truly be safe. Once Brinu knows I have escaped, he will send kobolds after me. And if he knows you are alive, he will do the same to you. You and I know too much to be allowed to live.'

Vender's eyes widened. 'Where can we go? How can we be safe?'

Lyell called Leaf over. She came gladly, huffing at him, and he stroked her neck. 'Where you go is your choice, Vender.'

'No, I'm coming with you,' said Vender. She murmured to Tail, and the salamander flitted up onto Leaf's head. 'I know where we should go.'

Lyell climbed onto the deer's back. 'Yes?'

'To Vaporcitta. To the humans. We should tell them what the elves did.'

Lyell gave a short, hollow laugh. 'They will kill me.'

'But what if you helped them?' said Vender. 'Helped them fight back. And anyway, who cares if it's dangerous? If you don't tell them the truth, then Brinu will make another disease to kill them all.'

Lyell hesitated. 'That is true. Lord Skytree won't rest until...'

'Then we should go,' said Vender. 'Or Tail and me could go.'

'No,' said Lyell. 'You have the disease, remember? If you went to the city, the other gnomes there would be infected.'

Vender's face fell. 'I feel fine.'

'But you are infected,' said Lyell. 'For now you should stay away. I can look after you until you're well again, if you want me to.'

'Then let's... let's wait awhile,' said Vender. 'Until we're ready to go back.'

12

—————

WHITEBARK

Lyell rode northeast, feeling the new strength in his limbs. His injuries were all gone now, or at least those on his body. His heart still hurt and it made his chest and throat tight with misery. Agafya was gone and she was never coming back. Her love had been the one thing left to him and now it was over. Finished. She would never love him again, even if he still loved her.

But at least she was alive. At least she knew the truth. And he could guess what she would be doing now.

The rocky ground grew more so as they went on, toward the outskirts of the forest. Near midday, they came across a river. It was deep and wide, its rushing waters studded with large chunks of stone. Leaf paused on the bank and then leaped, bounding from rock to rock with nimble ease. Lyell leaned with her, knowing balance was everything, and the deer reached the other side without stumbling.

Tail flew off ahead, but Vender stayed, clinging onto Leaf's ear. She didn't loosen her grip until they were safely on the far bank.

'Where are we going?' she asked at last.

'To a place none of my people ever visit,' Lyell said grimly. 'I would not go there myself if I had the choice. You will see it soon.'

Not far from the river, the trees began to thin out. They were different here, their trunks pale and smooth.

'Birch trees,' said Lyell. He eyed them with distaste. 'The birch is a cursed tree—its wood brings bad luck.'

'Why is that?' asked Vender. As usual, she sounded fascinated.

'You see the white bark?' said Lyell. 'White is the colour of bone. An unlucky colour. But now, here we are.' He pointed ahead.

The birches thinned out even further ahead, interspersed with rocky outcrops taller than Leaf. Beyond them was another wasteland. But this one was not burned like the one to the west, which the volcano Karvbac had created. The land here was grey and silver, filled with the bleached grey remains of dead trees. Even the sky seemed grey here.

Dead, brittle grass crunched under Leaf's hooves, and it too was grey.

'What is this place?' Vender breathed.

'This forest was once called Whitebark,' said Lyell. 'But now it is dead.'

'Did the elves ever live here?'

'Yes, there were elves here once,' said Lyell. 'Of a sort.'

Leaf trotted on through the dead forest. There was nothing here and not a hint of green to be found. There were no animals, either, other than the odd bird, and their presence only made the place seem greyer and more desolate. Lyell felt a chill down his spine at the sight. He had only come here once before, and that had been a very long time ago. Even Vender seemed subdued.

Finally, with evening drawing in, they reached the heart of Whitebark. Lyell had spotted it long before they came to it, but then a tree of that size was impossible to miss.

It towered over everything, just as the Skytree did, and it too was dead—long dead. Its bark had sloughed away, leaving nothing but grey wood.

Though the leaves were long gone, something still hung from the spreading branches, and Lyell winced internally at the sight. Even now, they were still here.

Bodies.

In life they had been the same size as him, and of a similar build. Now there was very little left of them. Only bones, held together by dried skin and sinew. They swung gently in the cold wind, the ropes creaking around their necks.

Vender gasped. 'What—what happened here?'

Leaf came to a halt, and Lyell slid off her back. 'This was another of the great trees; a brother to the Skytree. Those who once lived here called it the Worldroot. Some even said that it and the Skytree were offshoots of the same tree, the world tree, which holds all of Hylah in its branches. But the Worldroot died, as the Skytree has.'

'The people,' said Vender, still looking at the hanging bodies. 'What happened to them? Who killed them?'

'They were elves,' said Lyell. 'My people called themselves the golden elves. They were the silver elves, our cousins and rivals. When the Worldroot died, and their forest with it, those who survived came here to kill themselves. When I was young, my father brought me to see them, so I would know what might happen to our own people. Now we are the only elves left in Hylah.'

'That's so sad.' Vender looked away from them to Lyell's face. 'Lyell, why is this happening?'

'I don't know,' said Lyell. 'And perhaps Brinu was right.' He took hold of Leaf's reins. 'We should not stay here. This is a cursed place. We can find shelter further on.'

That evening they finally stopped in a small gully, where a large oak tree stood by a pool. It too was dead, but the hollow inside it was large enough to use as a shelter. Lyell took off Leaf's harness and left her to roam, and the deer started to browse among the dead grass, leaving him to set up a shelter.

Tail flew up to a low branch and perched there with Vender beside him, and while they rested Lyell went to the pool to refresh himself. Once he had drunk and splashed his face, he turned his attention to the tree. It had clearly been dead for at least as long as the Worldroot, but he should be able to work his magic on it. He wondered how different the process might be now he had become... whatever he was now.

He put his hands on the bark and felt for the tree's energy. It was there, if only faint and feeble, and it responded. Lyell put his energy into it, directing it to reshape under his hands. If he pitted the full strength of his magic against the tree, it should be enough to make the dead wood put forth a new branch and grow some acorns. That branch wouldn't live for long once his magic was gone from it, but—

Energy pulsed through Lyell, and it was far stronger than anything he had ever felt before. It poured into the dead oak in a torrent. Dry, dead sap began to flow and the tree creaked. Lyell looked up, bewildered, and saw the green energy and the wave of healthy new bark rippling away over the trunk, away from his hands. Up and out it went, and above him the oak's branches put forth fresh green leaves. Acorns sprouted in their cups, twigs sprouted and split, leaves spread wide in the dying light of sunset.

Lyell quickly pulled his hands away, but too late. It was done.

The tree was alive.

Vender gaped. 'You brought it back to life!'

Lyell stared at his hands, dumbstruck. Above him the tree sighed in the breeze, its healthy new leaves rustling.

'I didn't know you could do that!' Vender said with awe.

'I... have never done that before,' Lyell said slowly. 'I would never have had the strength. My magic...'

'You're stronger now,' said Vender. 'Whatever they did to you made you stronger. You can—' Her eyes widened again. 'Wait! Wait! If you can do that now, then maybe you can save the Skytree too—bring it back to life!'

Lyell caressed the oak's rough bark, he could feel the life inside it. Could magic truly be the answer? He had never heard of an elf with the power to resurrect a dead tree outside of legends. A slow, hot tendril of excitement began to twist in his chest.

'Yes,' he said. 'Yes, it could be possible. But I don't know how I would reach it. The Skytree is very well guarded.'

'Maybe you could try it here,' said Vender. 'With the Worldroot tree. If you can fix it, then you'll know it works.'

Lyell smiled to himself and got to work picking some acorns. 'I will try,' he promised.

The next day, Vender was sick. She woke up with agonising

pain in her chest and when she tried to speak all that came out was coughing. She coughed so hard she nearly fell from the branch where she had fallen asleep. Tail caught her and pulled her back. Vender clung to him, gasping for breath.

'*Friend, friend gnome,*' Tail rasped, his throat pulsating. '*Friend gnome sick?*'

Vender coughed again. '*Yes, yes sick,*' she managed to say. '*Bad sick.*'

Below them, Lyell emerged from his new home inside the tree. He was wearing a new tunic, shaped like a leaf, which he had woven from plant stems manipulated with magic, and his face was grim. 'Vender?'

Perched on the tree, head spinning, Vender looked down at him. 'Lyell, it's the sickness,' she whispered. 'My chest hurts.'

'Here.' Lyell held up his hands toward her.

Vender stepped unsteadily onto his palm and he lifted her down. Her chest was hurting worse than ever. She couldn't breathe. 'It hurts.'

Lyell held her gently. 'It will be all right,' he said. 'You will recover, I promise. I will take care of you until then—I owe you that.'

'Thank you.'

Lyell carried her into the tree and Tail flitted down after him. Inside he had made himself a simple bed of dried leaves, with a blanket woven in the same way as his tunic. He had also set up a bed for Vender: a niche in the wall, just the right size for her, with a blanket of her own.

'I thought you would need it soon, when the sickness came,' he told her. 'Do you like it?'

Vender managed to nod. Lyell crouched, holding her toward the niche, and she climbed out of his hand and into it, pulling the blanket over herself. It was soft and comfortable.

She pulled her hat off and put it under her head for a pillow. 'Thank you.'

'I will find the proper plants—you need medicine,' said Lyell. 'And I will gather some food for you. You should eat, to keep your strength up.'

Vender had no appetite, but she accepted anyway and let herself relax in her new bed. She was shivering, but she didn't feel cold.

After a while she drifted off to sleep, but it wasn't good sleep. It was full of horrible, confused dreams. She could feel herself trembling all the while, but she couldn't wake up.

When she finally did wake, it was dark and Lyell was there. He had lit a fire at the entrance to the hollow, and she caught the smell of food. It made her stomach churn.

'Here.' Lyell offered her a bowl made from an acorn cup. 'Drink this.'

Vender fumbled for it and drank. The medicine tasted sharp and sour, but she forced herself to swallow it. Afterward, Lyell gave her some water, which was much more welcome, and passed her a piece of the acorn bread he had made.

Vender chewed listlessly on it. 'I feel weak,' she said in a wheezy voice. 'I don't reckon I could even stand up anymore.'

'You will be fine,' Lyell assured her. 'Rest and medicine will give you back your health.'

Vender looked blearily at him. 'Lyell?'

'Yes, Vender?'

'What's going to happen to Agafya? Where has she gone?'

Lyell paused, and once again there was that sad, distant look she remembered from the first time she had met him. 'I think I can guess,' he said.

13

BURNING FOR REVENGE

Agafya found the last of them in the very place she had wanted to bring them all to: the ruins of Fivrath. She had sworn never to return to the city, but now... now there was no other choice. There was nowhere else they could go.

There wasn't much left of the city by now. Smoke still drifted from the cracks in the streets, but many of the buildings had fallen down and all were abandoned.

Agafya rode among them on her saurian Esfir. The others rode with her, respectfully keeping behind her. There were only a handful of them, but even so they were dwarves, and she had brought them back to their ancestral home.

She felt some joy at the thought, but it was a savage joy, and the sight of the surrounding ruins only hardened the hatred and anger in her heart. She saw the bones of the dead, lying where they had fallen, and there were so many of them... and not all of them were dwarves. Not far from the volcano itself, Esfir's claws crushed the dried remains of a kobold.

'You don't think there could be some hidden here?' one of her companions asked nervously.

'I am doubting that, Yevgeni,' Agafya answered. 'There is nothing here for them to eat, and the air would poison anyone not a dwarf. But...' She gritted her teeth. 'If any do attack us, then we will kill them.'

The others muttered agreement.

Yevgeni drew up beside her on his own saurian and looked up at the citadel. 'So strange,' he said. 'I never thought I would see it again, let alone ever go inside of it. A charcoal burner like me.'

Agafya smiled sadly. 'As the last of the Ivanos, I give you my permission,' she said.

She remembered the layout of the citadel carved into the volcano well and easily led them around to the side where there was an entrance for saurians. Normally it would have been guarded and protected by an iron gate, but now the guards were gone and the gate hung open. Esfir went in without prompting; she remembered too.

Agafya drew her axe and put her magic into the blades. They lit up at once, showing the way, and the others followed.

Beyond the entrance was a stable with stalls carved into the living rock. The stablehands were long gone, of course, so Agafya dismounted and took Esfir's harness and saddle herself. The saurian stumped away toward the nearest stall, obviously pleased to be home.

Once the others had dismounted, and the saurians were busy tearing at the chunks of meat their riders had brought with them on the journey, Agafya led the way into the citadel itself.

It was wonderfully hot here. Karvbac was a living volcano, full of fire. It was what sustained the dwarvish race. Everywhere outside its boundaries was cold and the air painful to breathe. Here, though, all was as it should be.

Agafya breathed deeply, savouring it, surprised to realise how happy she was to be here again. The rugged rock corridors twined around inside the mountain to the higher peaks where the living quarters were. They could talk when they reached the council hall.

But when Agafya reached the hall doors, they were closed and locked. Puzzled, she gave them a shove. They wouldn't budge. 'Why would it be locked?'

'Maybe whoever was last to leave locked it before they went,' Vitya suggested.

'But they only lock from the inside!' said Agafya. 'If someone locked it, then... they are still in there.'

'Then we will never open these doors,' said Yevgeni. 'If one of ours locked them and then died, then they—'

There was a sharp clanking sound, and the 'male' door swung open. On the other side was a dwarf man. He was middle-aged, and his ash-coloured hair was long and ragged. He stared at the newcomers in disbelief.

Agafya was the first to speak. 'Timur!' She lunged forward and hugged him as hard as she could. 'Timur, you live! You live!'

Timur started to laugh weakly. 'Agafya! After all this time... Where have you been? But come—come in!'

Inside the hall he had made a rough home for himself. His own saurian sat nearby, growling to himself, and Timur had tipped one of the stone council chairs on its side to serve as a slab bed. There were a few clay pots lined up against the wall beside it and a battered old axe.

'Have you been here all this time?' said Vitya. 'I thought you must have died.'

'I think that we all were thinking that of each other,' said

Timur. He waved at the circle of council seats. 'Sit. Have something to eat.'

With a faint lump in her throat, Agafya sat down on the seat that had once belonged to her mother. She glanced at the others. Four of them, five including herself. Once there had been thousands of dwarves in this city and now... only five.

Timur brought her some charcoal. 'It's not the finest, but still edible. But where have you been, Agafya? You disappeared that day...'

Agafya's jaw tightened. 'Yes, I ran from the city. I should not have. But now I have come back, and the time has come.'

'What time?' Timur sat and crunched on his own piece of charcoal. 'And where did you find the others?'

'We were living in the blasted lands,' said Vitya. 'But separately. I thought the others were all dead until Agafya found me. She persuaded me to come here with her. I think we are the only survivors.'

Timur sighed. 'I think that this must be the will of the gods,' he said. 'Our time has come to an end. But at least we are together.'

Agafya took a deep breath. 'Timur, Vitya, all of you, I must speak. There is something I must tell you.'

'What is it?' asked Yevgeni.

She paused, then squared her shoulders and began. 'It was not the will of the gods, what happened to us. It was the will of the elves.'

'What?' said Irina.

'I was the carrier,' said Agafya. 'I brought the sickness here. But I was wrong in thinking the disease was coming from the kobolds. It was the elves who infected me, and the ambassador, Lyell Blackfletch—' Her heart gave a hard, painful beat at the mention of his name, but she forged on. 'Lyell was here to make certain the city was struck down. The cures that did not work—he sabotaged them. That was his purpose. The elves wished to drive us to extinction. They sent the kobolds here to slaughter the last of us once the disease had done its work.'

They were all staring at her in disbelief.

'The elves?' said Timur. 'That cannot be true. They were our friends.'

'They betrayed us,' Agafya said bitterly. 'As Lyell betrayed me. I... I believed I was in love with him, and that he loved me. But now I know better. He confessed it, confessed everything. After he had overseen the destruction of Fivrath, he moved on to Vaporcitta and continued his work there. The human plague was their doing as well. Now they are even trying to bring the harmless gnomes to extinction.'

'No,' Irina breathed. 'It cannot be.'

'It is true,' said Agafya. 'All of it.' Her fist clenched around the piece of charcoal, crushing it into dust. 'They hope to destroy every other race in Hylah until only they are left. When Lyell...' She hesitated ever so briefly. 'When Lyell spoke out against it, his own people sentenced him to death. Now they will send a new ambassador to take his place, to finish his work in Vaporcitta.'

'And us?' Yevgeni asked sharply. 'What of us? What of the dwarves?'

'What of us?' said Agafya. 'The dwarves are finished. We five can never hope to bring our race back. Two women and three men... even if Irina and I both had children... it would not be enough. No, the dwarven race will end with us, or our children. All that matters to me now is revenge.'

Timur bared his teeth. 'Those filth! They betrayed us. And all this time I thought...'

Vitya leaped to his feet. 'I will see their forest burn!' he roared. 'Let us set it alight and drive the elves before us. They will see their home destroyed and they too will die!'

Yevgeni leaped up too, bellowing his approval, and so did Irina.

'Then so be it!' said Timur. 'We will go to war, one last time, and our last glorious act upon this earth will be to be seeing the elves punished!'

Agafya stood up. 'Wait!' she said loudly. 'Wait.'

They turned to look at her. 'Are you with us, Agafya?' Yevgeni demanded. 'Will you fight beside us?'

'I have a better plan,' said Agafya. 'Listen. We are not the only victims of the elves, no? The humans are too. I say we go to them. The humans were our allies in the past. We must ride to Vaporcitta and speak with the Chancellor. We will tell him the truth and offer our help. The humans have no magic, but they are having terrible weapons of their own. Together, we would see the elves destroyed.'

A brief silence fell, and then Timur thumped a big fist into his palm. 'A perfect plan! Once the humans know the truth, they will go to war and we will go with them. Silverwood will fall beneath us.'

'Let us do it,' Irina agreed. 'I have no fear. Not even the ravening kobolds will be able to hold us back.'

'Nothing will,' said Agafya. 'Nothing.' But even as she said it, hearing her own savage determination, something faint and sad stirred in her. *Lyell*, she thought. *My Lyell.*

14

VENDER'S QUEST

Vender's sickness took a long time to heal. She stayed in her bed for a week, coughing and shivering, often throwing up the food that Lyell brought her. But the medicines he made helped, and after days of feeling completely miserable she started to improve. Tail stayed close by, leaving her to hunt for insects and small animals but always coming back. It was good to have him there. He even lit the fire for Lyell in the evenings when Vender asked him to.

As for Lyell, he was often away during the day, and when he came back in the evenings, he looked tired. Vender was too tired herself to think much about that, but at the end of the week, when she finally felt strong enough to get out of bed, she spoke up.

'What were you doing while I was sick?'

The hint of a smile showed on the elf's solemn face. 'If you feel well enough for it, I can show you.'

'All right.' Vender stepped onto his hand, and Lyell lifted her up onto his shoulder. She sat down comfortably, holding onto a lock of his hair. It had grown back now and he didn't look much different from how he had when she first met him, except for the wood grain patterns on his arms and the bark patterns on his face.

Lyell ambled away from the oak tree, which was still flourishing, and back the way they had come to reach it. Vender still felt sleepy, and a little stupid, but before they had gone very far she began to guess at what he was going to show her and her heart lifted.

It was exactly what she had thought it might be.

There, at the centre of Whitebark, the Worldroot tree was alive again. Its bark had regrown and fresh green leaves rustled in the canopy. It was even flowering. The hanging bodies were gone.

Vender gasped at the sight. 'It's alive!'

Lyell put his hands on the trunk, leaning against it as if he had been running and needed to catch his breath. 'Yes,' he said. 'Every day I came here to feed it with my magic. It took time, and most of my strength, but it worked. The tree lives.'

Vender cheered. 'You did it! You saved the tree! And that means...'

'Yes,' Lyell said gravely. 'And perhaps with this power, I can save the Skytree—if I can reach it.'

Shortly after this, Vender's strength returned. She and Tail went flying again, exploring the dead forest beyond the oak. Before long her cough had stopped and she felt more vigorous than she had in ages.

But while Vender was growing stronger, Lyell was not. Every day he went back to the Worldroot tree, and every evening he returned looking more exhausted than ever before. Vender saw it clearly enough. The elf was growing thinner, his eyes began to look dull and sunken, his hair rough, and his voice low. She asked him what was wrong, but he said nothing—only that he was tired.

'You look sick,' Vender finally told him. 'You look really sick. What is it? Do you need medicine too?'

Lyell shook his head. 'The tree, it... needs me.'

Vender tensed. 'What happened to the tree? Is it still...?'

'You may as well see it,' said Lyell.

Vender needed no more encouragement. She got onto Tail's back, and the salamander flew for the tree, leaving Lyell to trudge after them. These days he walked more slowly than before.

Vender and Tail reached the tree first, and her heart sank when she saw it. Tail landed on an outlying branch, and Vender reached out to touch the nearest leaf. It came free in her hand and she turned it over, seeing the spreading patches of brown. Around her the others were no better. Every leaf on the tree was curling and turning brown, and more of them littered the floor. The outermost twigs were grey and brittle. Dead.

Below them, Leaf was busy feeding on dead grass and moss. Lyell arrived and put his hands on the tree's peeling bark, just as he had done to the oak.

Tail flew down to him, perching on an upraised root. Vender stayed on his back, all her attention on the tree. 'It's dying! It's dying again!'

Lyell didn't seem to hear her. He kept his hands on the trunk, and as Vender watched, he began to shake. He breathed in slowly, but it sounded painful, and then he began to cough; ugly, hacking coughs.

'Stop!' Vender shouted at him. 'Lyell, stop! You're hurting yourself!'

Slowly, Lyell relaxed and leaned against the tree, breathing harshly. His face had gone horribly pale. 'The tree,' he said. 'I can't save it. It's sapping my magic. Something is killing it, something I can't see. Something in the air, or the earth. I've been trying to heal it, but... it's too much.'

Vender took off her hat, twisting it in her hands. 'What are we going to do?'

Lyell sat down on another root. 'I don't know. Perhaps there is nothing to be done. Perhaps my people truly are doomed and nothing could ever have saved us.'

'But there has to be a way—' Vender began.

At that moment, Leaf's head went up. The deer looked back over her shoulder, toward the darkening forest, and gave a warning huff.

Lyell want to her at once. 'What is it, Leaf?'

Leaf huffed again and pawed at the ground, her nostrils flaring. Nearby, Tail began to hiss and slap his tail against the root.

Lyell stared off into the distance and tensed. 'Something is coming.'

Before Vender could speak, the dead undergrowth around them erupted, and dozens of huge, shaggy shapes came bursting into the clearing around the tree, as tall as Lyell and much heavier, covered in pitch-black shaggy fur. Their long fangs dripped with drool.

'Kobolds!' Vender shouted.

Lyell only hesitated for an instant. Even as the first of the kobolds charged at him, he snatched up a fallen branch and whirled around on the spot, smashing it over the creature's head. Beside him Leaf reared up, her sharp hooves lashing out at her attackers. Lyell's branch broke, but he stabbed the kobold with the sharp end, shouting, 'Vender! Run! Get away!'

Tail's head rose, and he started to hiss and puff out his sides. '*Fly!*' he said. '*Fly now!*'

A kobold came at them, even as the salamander started to beat his wings, Vender clinging to his neck. The creature's huge paw came crashing down on him, hurling the pair of them to the ground. Vender fell off Tail's back, landing with a bone-rattling thump. She got up in an instant and ran to help Tail. The salamander was already up and trying to take off, but the kobold was there, snarling, its serrated claws coming for them. Somewhere she could hear Lyell shouting as he fought on and her heart twisted. He was in trouble as Fiorella had been in trouble, and here she was, once again unable to help.

Everything seemed to slow down then. Vender looked around wildly, searching for a way out. The kobolds were everywhere—she was surrounded, and so was Lyell. But then she saw it. There, beneath the roots of the tree: a hole. And even though she was different from the rest of her kind, even though she had flown, Vender was still a gnome.

'*Tail!*' she yelled. '*Come, Tail! Hole!*'

She bolted toward it without a second glance, dodging the kobold's paw, and dived into the darkness. Tail followed, scrambling over the soft earth and down into the ground. The kobold came after them, thrusting its paw down the hole to try to grab them—Vender heard the scrabbling of claws and a hiss from Tail. But the hole was too small for them, and she ran down the tunnel beyond it, shoulders hunched. In moments her large eyes had adjusted to the gloom, and she could see the rough root-bound walls on either side. More roots hung from the ceiling, smacking against her face as she ran.

After a short distance, the tunnel suddenly opened up and

Vender found herself in a huge open space. It was full of roots, thrusting down through the ceiling and into the floor like pillars. The air was still and cool, full of the smell of earth and musty wood.

Vender stopped there, breathing hard, and Tail waddled over to join her, his wings trailing. There was a long, deep slash in his tail—ripped through the membranes he used for flying. He was hissing in pain.

'Oh, you poor thing.' Vender hugged him around the muzzle.

Tail licked her hand with his slimy tongue. *'Hurt. Hurt tail.'*

'I know, I'll look after it for you,' said Vender. She looked around—the cave went on for a long way and there was no sign of anything living down here. Another tunnel led away from it, sloping deep into the ground. 'Where does that go?' she wondered. She looked upward to where Lyell must still be fighting and her heart clenched. 'Lyell... There were so many kobolds, and he's weak from using all that magic. What if they kill him? What if...?'

Tail didn't answer. He lay down, still hissing, and breathed fire over his injury.

'Rest,' Vender told him. *'Rest here.'*

She left him there and hurried back up the tunnel. She could see the light up ahead. But the moment she came too close to the entrance, a great shaggy paw blotted out the light. Vender fell back, and even as she hurried out of reach she saw the paw pull back, scooping the soil away. Claws scratched at the tunnel entrance, furiously digging.

It dug too deep. As Vender retreated, hoping the kobold would give up, she felt the sudden ominous shifting in the walls. Dirt rained down from the ceiling.

'Stop!' she yelled pointlessly. 'Stop, you're breaking it!'

The kobold only dug on, destroying the tunnel. Vender turned and ran, just in time. The roots holding the walls together broke apart and the tunnel entrance collapsed. The kobold's paw withdrew, but when she went back to see what had happened, she found her way blocked by rock and soil. She started to dig through it, but the rocks had packed together so tightly that she couldn't shift even one of them.

She was trapped.

Numbly, she went back into the cave where Tail was waiting. 'The tunnel broke,' she told him. 'We can't get out.'

Tail peered in her general direction. He probably couldn't see in the dark the way she could. *'Fly?'* he suggested.

'No fly,' said Vender. *'No sky.'*

The salamander made a rasping noise.

Slowly, Vender turned to look at the other tunnel. 'We have to go that way,' she said, mostly to herself. 'Maybe that will take us out of here. But I hope Lyell is all right.'

There was no time to waste. The sooner they got out, the sooner they could find out what had happened to Lyell. Vender took a deep breath, adjusted her hat, and set off down the tunnel with Tail following.

15

IT BREAKS

The first time Agafya saw the human city, she was shocked.

It was huge—much bigger than she had expected—and the sky above it was thick with smoke. Massive pillars thrust into the air, belching smoke, and the River Wend here was filthy.

'Humans are repulsive creatures,' Yevgeni remarked. 'Look at the squalor they are living in. Inside the city, it even more foul.'

'You've been here before, yes?' said Timur.

'Long ago, yes. I doubt the humans will remember me. They live such short lives.'

Sure enough, when they entered the city Agafya saw just how filthy it was. Everything was encrusted with soot and the streets were strewn with garbage. There were a few birds about, but they looked sickly, their feathers dirty and greasy. Agafya grimaced at the sight.

The humans who saw them coming all stared, many of them wearing shocked expressions. She heard them shouting in their own language. 'Dwarves! They're dwarves! Dwarves in the city!'

'We are coming here to see the Chancellor,' Agafya said loudly, stumbling over the words a little. The human tongue was the one most races used to speak to each other, but it still felt awkward to her.

'This way!' a human said eagerly, and ran off ahead, showing her the way. Esfir and the other saurians lumbered after him.

By the time they reached the hall, the Chancellor was already at the door waiting for them. He was an aristocratic-looking human, finely dressed by the standards of his race, with cogwheel tattoos on his face. And behind him, staring impenetrably at the little group of dwarves, was an elf.

Agafya's breath hissed between her teeth and her heart gave a painful lurch at the sight of the tall, golden-eyed figure, but it was not Lyell. Of course it wasn't. This elf was a woman, with pale brown hair and a pattern of flowers tattooed on her forearm. But, like Lyell's, her face gave nothing away.

The Chancellor bowed politely to Agafya. 'Dwarves,' he said. 'Welcome! Welcome to Vaporcitta! I am Chancellor Albano Agano. This is such an honour. Forgive me, but we thought your people were all dead.'

'We are coming close to it,' Agafya growled. 'Very close.' She and her fellows were all openly glaring at the elf woman, who remained perfectly calm. 'Chancellor, I must be speaking with you alone.'

'Of course,' he answered. 'If you would—'

'Chancellor! *Chancellor!*'

They all turned sharply, just in time to see a small group of humans sprinting toward them, red-faced and gasping.

'Chancellor!' one of them shouted again. 'At the city's edge —an elf! Another elf has come!'

'*Chyort voz'mi!*' Vitya swore.

The elf woman tensed. 'Another elf?' she said.

'Yes, he's riding this way,' said the man, bowing to her. 'I think he's hurt.'

Agafya swore too. 'It can't be...'

Before anyone else could speak, they all heard the clatter of hooves. Heart pounding sickeningly, Agafya drew her axe as the deer came cantering toward them. And there, on her back...

'*Lyell!*' the elf woman hissed.

Leaf came to a halt, tossing her head and snorting, and Lyell slid off her back, stumbling when he hit the ground. His tunic was torn and there were traces of dried blood on it. He clutched at his side, wincing, and stared at Agafya. 'Agafya,' he rasped.

Agafya stared back, stunned, but then her eyes narrowed. '*You*,' she spat.

'Yes.' Lyell limped toward her, but now he looked past her at the astonished Chancellor. 'Albano,' he said. 'Chancellor. I must tell you—'

The elf woman pushed forward. 'Silence!' she snapped. 'Chancellor, Lyell Blackfletch is a traitor and an outcast. My Lord Brinu sentenced him to death, but he fled from his rightful punishment. He is mad. You must have him killed at once.'

Lyell barely spared her a glance. 'Chancellor, the elves have betrayed you,' he said quickly. 'The plague was of our making. It was I who stole the cure—'

The other elf froze, then pushed forward, shoving the dwarves aside. She drew a dagger and stabbed at Lyell, aiming for his heart.

Agafya shoved her away. 'Leave him!' she roared. 'He speaks the truth! The plagues were from you. You destroyed the dwarvish race, and you tried to destroy the humans, and the gnomes!'

Lyell moved back, and when the other elf tried to come after him, the dwarves seized her. She was taller than them, but they were stronger and they hurled her down at the Chancellor's feet. Agafya pinned her down with her axe, resting it against the elf's neck. 'Move and your head is mine.'

'Thank you.' Lyell leaned against Leaf's flank, breathing hard. 'She was here to carry on my work. Another plague will come, and she would have seen it destroy the human race. I came here to tell you that, Chancellor. I came to tell you the truth.'

The Chancellor said nothing—he looked too shocked to speak. But in moments the other humans who had gathered began to mutter.

'Lord Brinu is your enemy,' said Lyell. 'He tried to have me killed for refusing to destroy the cure. He sent kobolds to kill me when I escaped from my execution. They obey him.'

'It is true,' said Agafya. 'It is all true. What Lyell did to my people, he nearly did to you. We survivors are here to be offering you an alliance. We must fight back, all of us. The elves must be stopped.'

Lyell groaned. 'No—'

A rock flew out of the crowd and hit him hard in the back. He flinched, but made no attempt to defend himself. The humans began to shout, hurling accusations and abuse.

'Traitor! Murderer!'

The Chancellor's face darkened with anger. Behind him, his guards watched, waiting for an order. 'Betrayed,' the Chancellor muttered. 'And by the elves. By Vapora, I will

'Betrayed,' the Chancellor muttered. 'And by the elves. By Vapora, I will—'

'They must suffer for this. They must be punished!' Irina bellowed. 'I will see their forest burn!'

'No,' Lyell said again. 'Please, there must be—'

Nobody was listening to him now. The Chancellor made a short, sharp gesture at the men behind him. 'Guards—take the elves and lock them up at once. We will find out what they know.'

The elf woman struggled furiously, but Lyell did not. He sent Leaf away with a short command and allowed himself to be manacled and taken away. He cast one last sad look at Agafya and walked away between his captors, wincing as he put weight on his right leg.

'And so justice is done,' Timur said with satisfaction. 'I will be asking for the right to execute Lyell myself once you are done with him.'

'They will both be dealt with by the laws of human justice,' the Chancellor said coldly. 'This is my city. Now come—we have matters to discuss.'

The guards shoved Lyell into a cell, none too gently, and the barred door slammed shut behind him. He slowly lowered himself onto the bench provided, gritting his teeth at the pain. The wound on his side had not had time to heal and during the journey here it had stiffened and begun to throb with infection. Gingerly, he lifted his tunic and checked on it. The row of slashes over his ribs were ugly and swollen, crusted with greenish scabs. They needed to be drained, and soon.

Another door slammed, and Lyell glanced up. His fellow

elf had just been locked in the cell opposite his, where they could see each other. She was already at the door, wrenching at the bars.

'Let me out! This is an outrage. You cannot believe their lies!'

Lyell smiled thinly at her. 'I see your dignity has already fallen away from you, Nerith Bluecloud.'

She gave him a look of pure hatred and fury. '*You!* This is your fault!'

'Yes,' Lyell agreed. 'My fault. It was my fault the dwarves were destroyed, and my fault that the humans nearly died. Now, I have done my best to make amends.'

'You betrayed us!' she raged. 'You betrayed your own people! You are no elf. You... *dwarf lover.*'

Lyell flinched. 'My entire adult life, I have done wrong,' he said. 'Now I've done what was right. The time for lies is over.'

'The humans will still die,' Nerith told him. 'You know that. If the plague has failed, the kobolds will succeed. This foul city will be thrown into the sea. And you will die. The humans will torture you and then kill you.'

Lyell did not look away. 'You will die too, Nerith. But... I wish it did not have to be this way. What we did was evil, but I don't want to see our race destroyed. There are innocents in Silverwood.'

'And you should have thought of them,' said Nerith. 'You should have thought of them first, and not that filthy dwarf.' She spat through the bars. 'I know what you did. You *mated* with that creature. Don't lie. Degenerate. You may as well couple with a sheep, or a dog.'

Lyell's fists curled. 'Don't speak to me about her.'

'You are disgusting,' Nerith told him. 'Repulsive. You are no elf.'

'Then perhaps I don't wish to be,' said Lyell. He glanced away from her. 'Nerith, there is something I must tell you.'

'What?' She was still looking at him with complete contempt.

Lyell paused. Should he tell her? Yes, he should. Another elf should know. 'What was done to me in Silverwood changed me,' he said. 'I escaped the tree, but it is still with me, inside me.' He tapped himself on the chest. 'You can see the patterns of the wood on my skin. The Blackfletch tree—I own its power now. Its sap is in my blood, its wood in my flesh.'

Nerith paused. 'Truly?'

'Yes. It strengthened my magic. I have the power to raise dead trees to life. Even—'

Nerith's eyes widened. 'The Skytree? You could bring it back to us?'

'I tried.' Lyell coughed. The bad air was already beginning to affect him. 'I tried to heal the Worldroot tree. Its leaves grew green. It was alive. But then it died again. Something killed it.'

'Infection,' said Nerith. 'The filth and corruption of the lesser races. It killed the Worldroot just as it did the Skytree. But you...' She was looking speculatively at him now, her eyes narrow and calculating. 'If you have this power, then perhaps... it would be better for you to live. Once the land is cleansed, you could use this new magic to save the Skytree.'

Lyell hesitated. 'No.'

Nerith's eyes widened again. 'How can you say that?'

'If it means the destruction of every other race but our own, then my answer is no,' said Lyell. 'I would rather die.'

Her look of contempt came back. 'You truly are insane. But no matter, Lord Brinu will find ways to persuade you. Once we return to Silverwood...'

Lyell had heard enough. He turned away from her and fell

silent; there was no point in speaking of this any further. Neither of them were leaving this prison, not until it was time for their execution. He found himself unable to care much about that. After all, what did he have left to live for? Even poor, innocent little Vender had gone. He wondered what had happened to her.

'The gnomes are dying,' Nerith said suddenly. 'Did you know that? They are. We knew you would stop your little pet from returning to her kind, so we infected another. I brought him here with me. Now the little vermin are dying all through the city.'

Lyell looked up. 'You?'

'Yes,' said Nerith. 'A gnome ruined our plans here in Vaporcitta. It was time her race was cleansed from the land, from here, and in Bluedell.'

He gave her a long, slow look. 'Children,' he said. 'You are killing children, Nerith. The gnomes are a race of innocents, and because of you they are dying.'

'It is what must be done,' Nerith said stonily.

Lyell buried his face in his hands. So much death. The silver elves, the dwarves, the humans, and now the gnomes. And, soon enough, his own people as well. And why? For what?

For nothing, he thought. All for nothing.

16

WHAT LIES BENEATH

Vender had lost track of how long she'd been underground, but to her surprise she liked it better than she had expected to. There was something soothing about the gloom down here, and the smell of earth, and after a while she realised she had missed it.

Tail didn't like it much, but he fitted well enough, padding along the tunnel beside her. It was just the right size for a gnome, and Vender wondered if gnomes had actually made this place. But if they had, she couldn't see any of them, or any sign they'd been here.

There was food down here too—proper gnome food. She dug up grubs and edible roots, and the odd burrowing beetle, and shared them with Tail, who was kind enough to cook them for her. Vender munched away happily as they marched on. There was nothing better than roasted grub.

Still, she was starting to wonder just how far this tunnel went, and what would be at the end of it. Did it even *have* an end, come to that? Or would she come to a dead end? If that happened, she would have to try to dig her way out and she had no tools for that. It was scary, but exciting. She couldn't shake off the feeling that she would discover something down here. Treasure, maybe, or something even better.

'Wonder what happened to Lyell?' she said to Tail. 'I hope the kobolds didn't eat him. But I bet he got away—he's very strong. Maybe he went to look for Agafya.'

'*Dark,*' Tail complained. '*Dark here. No sky.*'

'*No sky,*' Vender agreed. '*Soon.*'

So far the air currents were telling her that there was more tunnel ahead and not a dead end. That was something, at least. But as they went on, that current began to grow stronger. Vender sniffed the air—it definitely wasn't as still as it had been before.

'There's a space ahead,' she said at last. 'A big space. I think the tunnel will end soon.'

She sped up, running one hand along the tunnel wall. A massive root was embedded in it, following the line of the tunnel. It had been there from the beginning, leading away from the Worldroot and on toward... whatever was ahead.

Finally, as she turned a corner in the tunnel, she saw it. Light. It was dim and flickering, but after so long in darkness it made her blink uncomfortably. 'Deep Spirit, look at that!'

Tail scurried forward eagerly, and Vender broke into a run behind him. At last!

The tunnel opened up into a huge cave, even bigger than the one under the Worldroot. The root they had followed all this way went beyond the end of the tunnel, curving down from the entrance. And there it met others. Great roots, thrusting out of the earth to meet at the centre, where there was a great knot of tangled wood. Some were huge, others smaller, but they all met at the same place, and the light was coming from there, deep inside that knot of roots. Green, pulsating, and magical.

Vender stared at it in wonder. 'What *is* this?'

There was more here than the knot of roots, much more. There were books, neatly stacked around the edges of the cave in shelves made from roots that seemed to have grown that way themselves. And there were bones. Thousands of them. Ribs and skulls littered the floor, bleached white like birch bark. The skulls were as big as herself, their eye sockets flickering in the light as if they were blinking.

'Deep Spirit,' Vender said again, blankly now. 'What? Why is this here? Who *are* they?'

At the far side there was a tunnel, many times larger than the one Vender had used, sloping upward. Maybe that could take her back to the surface. She didn't want to stay here. But even as she turned to speak with Tail, to tell him it was time to go, she saw movement. Someone was coming.

Vender hesitated, and then retreated into her tunnel, waving at Tail to come with her. He followed, and together they peeked out through the entrance as the stranger came into the cave. It was an elf, but it wasn't Lyell. It was another one Vender knew, and the sight of him made her breath catch in her throat.

'Brinu Skytree,' she whispered.

Brinu didn't know he was being watched. He wasn't looking at anything but the glowing knot of roots. Vender watched him, saw the look on his face. And she stayed where she was, and saw what he did next, and bewildered shock struck her in the chest like a fist.

~

The day after his arrest, Lyell sat in his cell and watched in resigned silence as a group of prison guards gathered by the door. Was it time at last?

But they had their backs to him as they opened the door to Nerith's cell. 'Get up,' one of them ordered. 'You're coming with us.'

Lyell stood and moved over to the bars to see what happened next. The guards manacled Nerith's hands together, despite her brief attempt to escape, and led her out of her cell and away down the corridor. Nerith's head held was high in a show of pride.

'Good luck,' Lyell muttered to her. In spite of everything, he felt some pity for her.

Hours passed. A meal of polluted human food arrived, and Lyell listlessly ate it. After some thought, he broke the clay plate it had arrived on and used a shard to open up the wounds on his side, grimacing as he scraped the muck away as best as he could. They had brought him some water and he used that to clean up. It was the best he could do.

As he was patting himself dry with a corner of his tunic, a faint dragging sound made him look up. Nerith walked between her guards as before, but now her head drooped and her footsteps were unsteady. He couldn't see any injuries on her, but there was a blankness in her eyes and a tightness to her mouth that told him all he needed to know. When her guards removed the manacles and pushed her into the cell, she stumbled and slumped onto the floor, breathing hard.

Lyell waited until the guards had left and watched as Nerith pulled herself up onto the bench. She was visibly shaking.

'Did you talk?' he asked softly.

Nerith leaned back against the wall, making a faint gasping

sound. Her hands twitched on her lap, and now Lyell looked closely he saw her fingertips were bloodied and mutilated. Every single one of her nails had been ripped out. He winced.

'I said nothing,' Nerith finally whispered, speaking their own language. 'Nothing.'

'It might be better if you did,' said Lyell.

Nerith did not reply. Lyell sat down and studied the wall of his cell, wondering grimly when his turn would come.

But when the next day came, he was left alone. They came for Nerith, hauling her away to face the interrogation room, and nobody so much as spared him a glance other than her. He caught the look of desperate fear in her eyes as they took her away, though she said nothing.

They brought her back that afternoon, and now she couldn't seem to stand up straight. Lyell watched her curl up on the bench, but he said nothing. After a while, she started to sob weakly.

The next day came, and once again Nerith was taken away while Lyell was left untouched. It made no sense. What were they going to do with him if not question him?

Either way, he was forced to see what became of Nerith. Over the course of that week, he watched her change. Before long she seemed to have forgotten how to talk and her eyes had taken on a fixed, blank look. She couldn't sit down without obvious pain and her hands no longer worked. Lyell saw the hideous bruising and suspected that they had been broken with a hammer or a vice.

Finally, one day, she broke her long silence and spoke to him in a dull flat voice.

'I talked.'

Lyell looked up at her. 'You told them?'

'Everything,' said Nerith, her tone not changing at all. She was staring at the wall of her cell, her gaze distant, as if she were in a trance. 'I told them everything. Skytree forgive me.'

'Then it's over,' said Lyell.

Nerith gave him an agonised look. 'I am a traitor. I am no better than you. Soon your turn will come.'

'Rest, now,' Lyell soothed. 'They have no more reason to hurt you now.'

She smiled a horrible, twisted smile. 'Even now... why do you speak kindly to me, Lyell?'

'Because you are one of my people,' said Lyell. 'And you are here because of me. Because of my betrayal.'

'Do you think I could forgive you?' Nerith asked bitterly.

'No,' said Lyell. 'And it was necessary. Your capture will save lives.'

Nerith's eyes grew hard. 'You are callous, Lyell. Callous and cruel.'

Lyell smiled coldly at her. 'I have had many long years of training in that, Nerith. To see another's suffering and do nothing—that was my good work for Brinu.' He rubbed the wounds on his side; they, at least, were healing now.

That was his last conversation with the other elf. An hour or two later they came for her again, and this time she did not return.

Shortly after that, Lyell's turn finally came. He stood up resignedly as the guards opened his door. 'I will go with you.'

They put the manacles on him and he went with them without complaint, but they took him in the opposite direction to Nerith, back the way he had come on his arrival and out into the city. He emerged blinking, puzzled. Were they taking him directly to execution?

But no, they marched him toward the Chancellor's hall, past other humans who hurled rotten fruit and screamed abuse. Lyell hunched his shoulders and did not look at them. They reached the hall and went inside, and there Lyell was taken to the Chancellor's study. The Chancellor was there, sitting at the table, and with him were Agafya and Timur. Lyell's stomach lurched at the sight of Agafya, but he gave nothing away. The dwarf's fists clenched as he came in and she gave him a look of pure hatred.

With a heavy heart, Lyell sat down on the chair as the guards directed him to, manacled hands resting in his lap. 'Chancellor,' he said. 'I know what I have done was unforgiveable. My execution will be justified, and I accept it.'

The Chancellor leaned forward, hands resting on the table. 'Yes, you have earned a death sentence, both here and in Fivrath. However, I must acknowledge that we also owe you a debt. If you had not disobeyed your lord and allowed us to keep the cure, the plague would have destroyed all of Vaporcitta. The human race still lives, thanks to your change of heart.'

Lyell paused. 'Gratitude?' he said. 'For me? No, do not thank me, Albano. I did what I could to atone for my crimes, but nothing can wipe them away. My blood is yours. Do what you wish with me.'

He had said all he had to say and he fell silent, waiting to find out what would happen to him. He didn't stop to ask about Nerith—he already knew she was dead.

'Yes,' the Chancellor said after a while. 'We have decided what to do with you, but you won't be executed. We have another use for you.'

Lyell looked up. 'What is that? Do you want me to fight for you? I am not a fighter, but I have my magic... If there is something I can do, ask and I will do what I can.'

'You would be calling yourself our ally, elf?' Timur butted in.

Lyell hesitated. 'I have a debt to repay, to you and to the humans. My own people will never allow me to return to them. I am an outcast, as Nerith said. What do I have left, but to do what I can for you? So, I am your ally, for whatever that is worth.'

'Very well,' said the Chancellor. 'We have a task for you. Under interrogation, your friend Nerith revealed that you have the power to revive dead trees. Is this true?'

'Yes, it is,' said Lyell. 'I revived the great Worldroot tree in Whitebark, and it stayed alive for a time.'

'If that is true, then here is your task,' said the Chancellor. 'You will return to Silverwood.'

A knot formed in Lyell's chest. 'You would be sending me to my death,' he said.

'Perhaps so, perhaps not,' said the Chancellor. 'Speak with Lord Brinu Skytree. Tell him that you have the power to save the Skytree. If you succeed at it, then perhaps you will earn the forgiveness of your people.'

Lyell's throat grew tight. 'I could try...'

'Do so, then,' said the Chancellor. 'And once you have their trust, you will assassinate Lord Brinu.'

Lyell stared at him.

'That is your great work, yes?' said Agafya, speaking for the first time. 'To stab others in the back? Now you will do it again, for us.'

Lyell looked sadly at her. 'Yes, Brinu ordered my execution, and he ordered me to do the terrible things I did. I have no love for him. If you want me to kill him, then I will try. I can't promise that I will succeed, but I will try.'

'Good,' said the Chancellor. 'That will do. You'll have an escort to take you back to Silverwood. You leave immediately.'

Lyell looked at Agafya, then at him. 'Chancellor...'

'Yes? What is it? Speak quickly.'

'I wish that there was another way to resolve this,' said Lyell. 'If the Skytree lived again and Brinu were removed, then my people could live on and all of this would end.'

'It will end when the elves are dead,' Agafya spat. 'And you, Lyell—I promise you this. The next time I see you, I will kill you.'

'There will be no negotiation with your people,' said the Chancellor. 'This is war. The elves must be removed.'

Lyell hadn't looked away from Agafya. 'Then you would make yourself no better than them,' he said softly.

'That's enough,' said the Chancellor. 'This meeting is over. Guards, take him out of here.'

Lyell stood up, chains clinking, but before he left he looked at Agafya, looked her in the eye. 'Agafya,' he said. 'I love you. I love you with all my heart and I always will. It was your love that changed me, and I can never forget that. And the next time we meet... I will not resist. My life is yours to take, and yours alone. I will try to stay alive until then. At least that way I will see your face one last time.'

Agafya rose from her chair. 'Lyell...'

Lyell said nothing more. He smiled at her and left.

17

REDEMPTION

Lyell's escort was mostly made up of humans—ten armed soldiers, mounted on their own steeds: machines that looked something like horses, but made from metal, their flanks covered in exposed cogs. Smoke and steam rose from their nostrils and they made a constant clanking, grinding sound as they moved, their huge copper-plated hooves thudding on the ground. They looked clumsy and lumbering, but Lyell knew they could move with shocking speed if it came to it.

Leaf did not like the machines at all—she kept her ears back and shied whenever one of them came too close to her. Lyell patted her on the neck and murmured to reassure her. She had waited for him outside the city, as she always did.

Timur had come too. He rode at the back of the group on his saurian, which kept hissing and showing its serrated fangs. The dwarf had his sword close to hand, and all the humans carried the clockwork rifles they used. Lyell had been told that if he tried to escape, he would be killed immediately, but the threat had been unnecessary.

Lyell had no intention of fleeing. There was nowhere else

to go now, and besides, the thought of killing Brinu was a powerful temptation. And if he failed, then at least he would be allowed to die in Silverwood, where he belonged.

They travelled in silence—naturally nobody wanted to speak to him, and he had nothing to say to them. He spent his time thinking instead, choosing what he would say when he faced his lord again.

Meanwhile, they took the same route to Silverwood as Lyell had used the last time, following the river. Soon enough they reached Como, and the people came to meet them at once.

'My Lord Lyell!' one of them said in surprise.

Lyell said nothing, but he inclined his head politely toward him.

The captain in charge of the soldiers pulled a lever on the neck of his horse, which ground to a halt. 'People of Como,' he said in a loud voice. 'By order of Chancellor Albano Agano, you must leave. Evacuate to Vaporcitta immediately. You will be given shelter there.'

They exchanged glances.

'Why, sir?' asked the man who had spoken first. Lyell recognised him—Figaro.

'Como will soon be under attack,' the captain told him. 'Another plague will come, or there will be a kobold attack.'

'It will be kobolds,' Lyell said suddenly. 'The plague has failed. Now Brinu will try to destroy your race by less subtle means.'

Figaro stared at him. 'What?'

Timur growled. 'Tell them, elf.'

Lyell nodded curtly. 'The elves are your enemies. They... *we* created the plague, and the kobolds obey us. You must go to Vaporcitta for sanctuary.'

Cries of shock and outrage rose from the crowd. 'It was *you?*' said Figaro. 'You did this to us?'

'Yes, and to many others,' said Lyell. 'But there is no need to be afraid of me now. I am a prisoner.'

The shouts grew louder, but the captain called for silence and finally got it. 'Enough,' he said. 'Collect your belongings. You must leave by tomorrow. The elf will be dealt with.'

They rode on without another word, but though the people let them go, some threw mud or rocks at Lyell. Mud splattered over his hair, and he flinched but otherwise ignored it, though he could still hear Timur's loud, scornful laughter.

Strange, he thought as they left Como behind. *The last time I came this way...*

But now the truth was out, there would be no more awestruck respect from the humans, or anyone else for that matter. He may as well get used to being abused like this.

He wondered, with curious detachment, how much longer he was going to live. He had escaped death several times already, and sooner or later his luck would run out. He could only hope he fulfilled his mission first, and that he could keep his promise to Agafya. Perhaps killing him would bring her some kind of peace, or at least satisfaction. He owed that to her.

Some way out of Como, they passed through another place Lyell remembered.

Bluedell.

The solitary house was there, not too far from the river, and by now the surrounding garden had grown wild. The windows were smashed, the door broken in, and he could see the deep slash-marks in the frames.

'Kobold attack,' one of the humans muttered. 'This was where the Chancellor's sister lived. This was her country cottage.'

'Then she made the cure here,' said one of his colleagues. 'That little gnome, Vender—they lived here together before—'

'Wait.' Timur urged his saurian forward, past the steadily ticking horses. The dwarf pointed. 'Look there, by the riverbank.'

Lyell winced at the sight of the small, crumpled body that lay collapsed on the mud. 'A gnome,' he muttered.

Timur slid off his mount and walked over to the gnome, which stirred feebly. 'He lives.'

'Poor little thing,' said one of the humans.

Timur gently picked the gnome up and carried him back to the group. It was a man, pale-skinned and big eyed, as gnomes generally were, and there was something about his pointed chin and light brown hair that looked familiar to Lyell.

'Hello, gnome,' the captain said cautiously. 'Are you hurt?'

The gnome coughed—once, twice, and a third time, and his small body convulsed. Blood foamed around his mouth. 'Sick, I'm real sick,' he wheezed, looking up at them with an expression of pathetic bewilderment. 'Every gnome, they all right sick. Our father, he slept and didn't wake up. My sisters, my brothers...'

Lyell's insides crumbled. 'What is your name, gnome?'

The gnome coughed again. 'Bramble. Bramble Bluedell. My head be right sore.'

Timur gave Lyell a look of pure venom. 'Even them,' he growled. 'Is there nothing your kind won't stoop to?'

Lyell did not reply. 'Bramble,' he said. 'Were you in Silver-wood? Did you see the elves?'

Bramble nodded feebly. 'Yes, yes—they asked for me. The elves be kind to me. But that kobold...'

'You will live, Bramble,' Lyell told him. 'The carrier... always lives.'

'But lives for what?' Timur said bitterly. 'Lives to see his people die, the way Agafya did? Death would be better.'

The captain waved him into silence. 'We will take care of him. Elf, is there a cure? This plague—do you know the way to cure it?'

Lyell shook his head. 'We create the disease, not the cure. There is no need…' he trailed off. 'Bramble, do you know another gnome named Lavender?'

'Yes, yes, Lavender be Bramble's sister,' said Bramble. 'The crazy one.' He broke off into another coughing fit. 'Kobolds ate her.'

'No,' said Lyell. 'Your sister is alive. And maybe you will see her again. If I find her, I will tell her where you are.'

Bramble's eyes widened. 'For true?'

'For true,' Lyell promised. 'Your sister is my friend.'

Saying it felt good.

'Enough,' the captain interrupted. 'We must move on. Officer Nevio, take care of the gnome.'

'Yes, sir.' The soldier took Bramble with surprising gentleness and settled him down in the saddlebag in front of him.

Lyell looked ahead toward the looming mass of Silverwood and felt apprehension twinge in his chest, but there was more than fear there, and it was enough to harden his resolve. There was hatred, and it was deep and strong and burning for revenge.

At the edge of the forest, the group came to a halt.

'Go, elf,' the captain said brusquely. 'And may the Pantheon forgive you if you fail.'

'I will not fail,' said Lyell. 'Brinu will die. I will bring you his head.'

'Come back without it and I will be killing you,' said Timur.

Lyell looked him in the eye. 'No, Timur. Remember my promise. My life is Agafya's to take. Farewell.' He urged Leaf forward and the deer trotted away into the trees, happy to return home. Lyell felt their stares on the back of his neck as he left, but he did not look back. The only way now was forward.

Somehow he had expected to be intercepted the moment he entered the forest, but there was nothing. It was as quiet among the trees as always. Lyell breathed deeply, glad to taste the pure air once again. The magic inside him thrummed, revitalised by the presence of healthy trees and clean water. Leaf snorted and nibbled at some lichen that hung from a branch. Lyell plucked some as well and chewed on it as they went uphill toward the waiting Skytree. Soon enough, he would see it again.

They reached the edge of the clearing unmolested, but Lyell had already seen them: a large gathering of elves, sitting or standing among the roots. The Skytree's trunk was grey and peeling, its leaves all but fallen, and even though he had known it would be that way the sight still thumped sickening shock into his stomach.

He brought Leaf to a halt and dismounted. 'Go,' he whispered to her. 'You can rest now.'

The deer nuzzled his shoulder and wandered off into the trees. Alone, Lyell stepped into the clearing, his hands up to show he was unarmed. 'Brinu!' he called.

The elves sprang upright and began shouting. 'Lyell! It's the traitor! *Lyell!*'

They said his name as if it were poison.

Fear stabbed at Lyell, but he did not move. 'Brinu!' he said again. 'My Lord, I must speak with you. Something terrible has happened. You must be warned.'

They were on him in a moment. Six elves rushed at him, and Lyell took a quick step backward, but in an instant he was surrounded. Vicious blows struck him in the face and chest, hurling him to the ground. He landed with a thump and a groan and curled up as they started to hit him, kicking him in the stomach and ribs. The barely healed wound in his side split open and began to bleed.

'Kill him!' people were screaming. 'Kill the traitor!'

Lyell covered his head with his arms. 'Stop!' he shouted. 'They are coming. The humans are gathering! They know the truth—the dwarves...'

And then, mercifully, Brinu was there. 'Stop!' he commanded. 'Let him go.'

The elves stopped beating Lyell and most of them backed off, but two pulled him up by his shoulders. He hung between them, gasping. His nose was bleeding, sap-filled blood dripping onto his scarred chin. He tried to get up, but they forced him to stay down, kneeling in front of his ruler.

Brinu's face was dark with anger and suspicion. 'What is this?' he said. 'Speak quickly, traitor.'

Lyell coughed. 'My Lord, I am sorry. I was wrong. I went in search of the dwarf Agafya, to dispose of her as I was meant to—she knew too much. I killed the gnome, but Agafya escaped. She gathered the other dwarves who survived the plague. I chased them to Vaporcitta, but I was too late. They told the humans the truth about us. Nerith and I were both arrested.'

Silence fell.

'Humans!' Eala spat. 'Those scum! Where is Nerith?'

'Dead,' said Lyell, wincing. 'She and I were both tortured. She broke and told them everything they wanted to know. They executed her afterward. Now they plan to attack Silverwood, and they have allied with the dwarves. They mean to burn the trees and slaughter every one of us. I escaped. I knew I must warn you.'

The other elves groaned aloud. 'Humans, coming here?'

'They will never reach us!' Kiya scoffed. 'The kobolds will destroy them.'

'Yes, they must be gathered,' said Lyell. 'But my Lord, there is more.'

'Yes?' said Brinu. 'Are you hoping to escape your proper punishment by bringing me this news, Lyell?'

'No,' said Lyell. 'But there is something I can do. My magic —it has grown stronger since you gave me to the tree. Please, let me show you. I must touch the Skytree.'

Brinu paused. 'What is this? What are you saying?'

'I am saying I can save the Skytree,' said Lyell.

The others began to murmur. 'You? *You* believe you can do this?'

'I think so,' said Lyell. 'I brought the Worldroot back to life in Whitebark. I could do the same for the Skytree.'

'Release him,' Brinu said abruptly.

The elves holding Lyell pulled him to his feet and let him go. Lyell wiped the blood off his nose; everyone was staring at him now, wide-eyed as Bramble had been. There was anger there, and deep suspicion, but there was terrible hope as well.

Lyell took a deep breath. It was now or never. If he failed, he would die. Even success might kill him.

He limped over to the Skytree and put his hands on its trunk. He could feel the faint pulse of life in the wood—the tree wasn't completely dead after all. He braced himself and felt his magic flow.

Energy rushed out of him and into the tree, more powerful than ever, and Lyell gasped at the sensation. His head snapped up and he saw the fresh bark spreading away from him. Behind him the other elves had begun to shout. Some even screamed.

Lyell did not stop. Teeth gritted, he put his full strength into the task, even when it began to hurt. Sap pounded through his veins and his skin began to feel stiff and wrong, the sensation leaving it. His vision wavered. Above him the Skytree's leaves burst free, green and perfect, and pain spiked in Lyell's back and arms as something thrust out through his skin.

Around him the others cried out in ecstasy and wonder. Then, one by one, they began to sing—a high, haunting song to the glory of the tree.

Lyell's throat felt as if it was full of bark. His senses were fading now, but he couldn't seem to pull his hands away from the tree, couldn't seem to—

Then, abruptly, everything went black. Some powerful force dragged Lyell away from the tree. He felt the thump as he hit the ground, and after that—nothing.

He woke up some time later, feeling hideously weak but warm. There was a faint murmuring of voices around him. And singing. Laughter.

Lyell forced his eyes open and found himself looking up at a sighing canopy of perfect leaves. The Skytree's leaves covering its spreading branches. It was alive. Alive and as magnificent as it had been when he was a boy.

Lyell did not move. He lay there and stared at it, and tears slowly began to run down his face. He had done it.

A gentle hand touched his arm. 'Lyell.'

Lyell glanced over at Eala's smiling face. 'I did it,' he whispered. 'The Skytree... it lives.'

'Yes, Lyell. You saved it. You saved the elvish race, and you saved our home.'

Lyell smiled back at her. 'Yes... yes, I did.'

Others had noticed he was awake and they came over in ones and twos. There was no hatred in them now, no suspicion —only radiant happiness.

'How do you feel?' asked one of the men.

'Weak, but I think I will recover,' said Lyell. He looked down at himself. Someone had put a blanket over him, but one of his arms lay on top of it and he blinked in surprise: he had sprouted leaves. Little fleshy growths peppered his skin and each one had budded into a leaf. The leaves of the Blackfletch tree.

'You truly are one with your tree,' Kiya said in wonder. 'You were in it, and now it is in you.'

'Yes.' Lyell freed his other arm with an effort and tugged at one of the leaves. It came free with a little trickle of sap and blood. 'I wonder if I will drop my leaves in autumn?' he said aloud.

The others laughed. 'Perhaps you will,' said someone. 'Truly, there has never been anyone like you, Lyell Blackfletch.'

'Am I forgiven, then?'

'Yes.' Brinu came to crouch beside him. 'Yes, you are forgiven, Lyell. You may make your home here again. Your sentence of death is revoked. You made a mistake, but now you have redeemed yourself for that. Now, rest. You will be taken care of.'

'Thank you,' Lyell mumbled.

He slept for a while after that, and when he woke up, he felt better. With some help from Eala he sat up, and they helped him over to the fire. The others had prepared a feast, and Lyell ate ravenously, surrounded by the joyful faces of his people. Ardrathar Rocktree and Tarnya Rivertwist had hunted down a couple of fine deer, and Kiya had brought a brace of rabbits. Others had gathered fruits and vegetables, and Eala had even come across a beehive and collected some honey.

Every elf in Silverwood was here now. Men, women, and a few precious children. Elves had always been slow to reproduce, so there had never been many children in Silverwood, but now there were even fewer than there had been before. The death of the Skytree had brought down the curse of infertility, and there were now only seventeen children among hundreds of adults.

Lyell watched them at play, climbing over the roots of the Skytree and talking in their high, piping voices, and guilt sickened him. They didn't deserve to be caught up in this, any more than Vender had deserved it. But how could anyone protect them?

Finally, he dared to speak up. 'So,' he said, noting how everyone stopped to listen, 'perhaps I was right. The Skytree lives, even though Hylah has not been... cleansed.'

Silence fell.

'You could be right, Lyell,' Tarnya said grudgingly. 'Perhaps now that the Skytree lives again, it won't be necessary to complete our sacred task.'

'No,' said Brinu. 'The lesser races must still be removed. Now that the Skytree has returned to life, our strength will return with it. We will be strong enough to do what must be done. Once Hylah is cleansed, the forest will spread. Trees will grow where the human city once stood, and the other great trees will be restored. Soon enough, we will be free to live in the proper way, without the corrupting influence of those creatures.'

Lyell's heart sank. 'And the kobolds?'

'They will serve their purpose and destroy the humans,' said Brinu. 'After that, they will be disposable. Put your mind at ease, Lyell—all will be well.'

Lyell looked at him, narrow-eyed. *Yes,* he thought. *Soon enough, it will be.*

18

STUMPS

The humans were gathering. Agafya watched it all with grim satisfaction, walking the streets of Vaporcitta and witnessing their preparations for war. There were fewer of them now than there had been before the plague, of course; she could tell by the number of abandoned houses and empty shops. But there were still far more of them than she had expected, and more were pouring in. Humans were short-lived, but they bred quickly, and at the Chancellor's command they were leaving their towns and villages and coming to the city. They were given new homes, in houses whose owners had been killed in the plague, and the men were ordered to report to the barracks for training. The human army was growing, and it was thousands strong, armed with the terrible weapons their kind had invented and fuelled by hate.

Against them, she knew, the elves would not stand a chance.

She went by the barracks and watched the humans in the training yard. They were hard at work, being drilled by a man who was showing them how to handle clockwork pistols and rifles. Pistolmen at the front, riflemen at the back.

'Forward!' the officer roared. 'Crouch! And fire!'

A volley of loud cracking bangs split the air, and dust and shards of wood puffed away from the targets. Agafya nodded to herself, unsmiling. Humans understood discipline; they fought with precision, like the machines they built. The dwarves had never been like that. But perhaps human numbers and discipline would help them win this. As for Agafya, she was more than prepared to accept the direction of the human commanders. She had never been in a battle before, but the humans had, and they would know what her best use would be. For now, she had to wait.

She left the barracks and wandered off into the city. It was interesting to explore the place, though she still didn't understand how the humans lived surrounded by this much garbage, and with a river so thick with oil and other waste. Still, it was fascinating. The humans had no magic, but they had used their ingenuity to build so many astonishing things. Perhaps that was their power.

Now Agafya headed for the Temple of the Pantheon, where the humans worshipped. She had always wondered what it was like inside.

There was plenty to see along the way. She passed by the marketplace, used to the curious stares of the humans, and wandered by the river, where massive factories lined the waterfront. Smoke belched from the stacks above and pipes jutted into the water, spilling a constant stream of oil and other liquids she did not recognise, though they smelled noxious.

'Dwarf!'

Agafya looked up and smiled slightly. 'Yes, little one?'

The human child skidded to a halt, staring at her with fascination. 'Are you a dwarf? Really?'

'Yes,' said Agafya. 'My name is being Agafya Ivano. And you?'

The child, a girl, bit her lip. 'I'm Amalia. Do you know medicines?'

'No,' said Agafya. 'Why are you asking, Amalia?'

The girl opened up the bag she was carrying. A gnome was huddled down inside, wheezing pathetically. 'Grass is sick,' the girl said solemnly. 'I'm trying to take care of him, but he won't get better. Do you know how to make him better?'

Agafya looked sadly at the little creature. 'No,' she said. 'I am sorry. But the human healers are finding a cure.'

'But what if Grass dies?' said Amalia, tears on her face. 'I don't want him to die—he's good. He's my friend.'

'All you can be doing for now is to take care of him,' said Agafya. 'Make him comfortable and keep him warm.'

'I will,' said Amalia. She still looked deeply unhappy. 'Grass's family died. All the gnomes are dying.'

'I know,' Agafya said grimly. 'This is what the elves did to them, and to my people. But they will not be doing it to your people.' She paused, seeing the girl was about to cry, and said, 'Do you know what I am thinking?'

'What?' Amalia sniffled.

'The time of the dwarves is over,' said Agafya. 'Soon enough the last of us will die. But the elves will die too. We will destroy them. They can never do this evil again. I think that after that, the future will belong to your kind. To the humans. When that day comes, it will be being your responsibility to care for Hylah. You must be ready for that. But can you promise me something, Amalia?'

She nodded eagerly. 'What promise?'

'Promise that you will always remember us. The dwarves and the gnomes, and everyone else who is gone. That way we will never truly die.'

'I promise,' said Amalia.

'Now, I must be going,' said Agafya. She paused. 'Can you show me to the temple?'

'I will.' Amalia checked on Grass, but the gnome was clearly asleep, his face glistening with sweat.

The temple wasn't too far. Agafya followed the child with a heavy heart, though she was careful not to let her sadness show. Everywhere in the city gnomes were dying, and in all likelihood they would be wiped out before a cure was found. Nerith had probably disposed of the carrier before Agafya and the others arrived. The elf's cursed head was hanging from the city walls by now, so justice had begun to be done.

Agafya tried not to think of Lyell, but she failed. His face would not leave her mind, and nor would that last sight of him, his face, his voice, the quiet way he had promised her that his life was hers to take. And she would take it. The next time she saw him, she would kill him. She would hack his head off with a blazing axe, and her race would be avenged.

Her jaw tightened, and she unconsciously reached down to touch her axe. *My Lyell.*

'Here,' said Amalia, interrupting her thoughts. 'It's here.'

Agafya looked up. The temple building wasn't too far from the Chancellor's hall, and though it was smaller than the factories, it was still impressive. It was a pillared building, made from pale stone, and the entrance was semicircular, edged with teeth like a cogwheel. Amalia went in first, bowing and murmuring at the threshold before stepping through it. Agafya followed.

Inside was a long hallway, lined with more pillars

protecting little shrines. At the far end there was something huge and roughly rounded, like a giant pillar that had snapped off at the base. It had been ringed in by a fence made of hundreds of gold and silver cogwheels welded together.

Agafya looked at it, both impressed and puzzled. 'What is that?'

Amalia pointed to the shrines on either side. 'Those are shrines to the different gods. That one there is Vapora, the goddess of steam.'

'But what is *that*?' said Agafya. 'That thing behind the fence.'

'Oh.' Amalia hurried toward it, carefully holding her bag so it wouldn't swing. There was another shrine by the fence—a plinth with a dish of clear water resting on top of it. Amalia opened her bag, and gently dabbed some of the water onto Grass's forehead, murmuring a prayer.

Agafya looked up at the thing behind the fence. It was the size of a human house, its sides rugged and blackened. There was something vaguely familiar about the shape, but surely it couldn't be...

'This is the shrine to Vitalo, the god of growing things,' said Amalia. 'He brings good health if you pray to him.'

Agafya put a hand on the fence, still staring at what lay behind it. It was so close she could touch it—and she did, poking a hand through a gap to brush it with her fingertips. A chunk of it came loose, and she pulled it out and examined it. Charcoal.

Amalia gaped at her. 'You can't touch it! It's forbidden!'

Agafya ignored her. 'This,' she said. 'This is a tree! This was a great tree...'

'Yes, it was called the Greatleaf tree,' said Amalia. 'But it's dead now. The people from the past cut down all the trees, and the Greatleaf tree died, so they cut it down and burned it. But they built the temple here because it's sacred. Nobody's allowed to touch it.'

'Hah.' Agafya stuffed the lump of charcoal in her mouth and crunched blissfully on it. It was very good quality.

Amalia looked even more horrified than before. 'You can't do that!'

'Thank you for showing this to me,' said Agafya, still unmoved. 'Soon the Skytree will be like this—a charred stump. Maybe I will eat some of that too,' she added coldly.

Two days later, while Agafya was relaxing in her room at the hall, Timur returned. He and the soldiers who had left with him came close on the heels of the refugees from Como, and when word reached her, Agafya hurried down to the meeting room to see him.

Timur nodded briefly to her. '*Privyet*, Agafya.'

'*Privyet*, Timur.' Agafya sat down.

The other dwarves joined them, along with the Chancellor's offsider Biagio and General Paolo Lacolo, the commander of the human army. The moment they were all there, Timur said, 'It is done. The elf has returned to his forest. Now we can only hope he does as he promised he would.'

'If not, then his people will kill him,' said Biagio. 'If he chooses to warn them about us...'

'We must attack quickly, and ruthlessly, before they have a chance to prepare,' General Lacolo interrupted. 'The reports from my scouts say that the kobolds are still roaming in loose packs. Together they will outnumber us, but we will have discipline and weaponry superior to theirs. I am confident that we can defeat the beasts.'

Timur leaned forward. 'And us? What will our role be?'

'You will be very important,' said the General. 'All five of you. When the time comes to attack Silverwood itself, your fire will be our greatest weapon. Let my men take the brunt of the fight against the kobolds. You will have something more important to do.'

'Tell us the plan,' said Vitya. 'We are at your command, General.'

'We will leave the city and march on the forest,' he replied. 'Our scouts will keep watch for the kobolds, of course. Most likely we will have to fight them before we come to Silverwood, unless they plan to ambush us there among the trees. Either way, when we reach the forest, part of the army will leave us and you will go with them. Skirt around the edges of the forest and unleash your fire at the rear of their settlement. Set the forest ablaze and drive the elves before you. They will be chased out into the open where the rest of us will be ready for them. Among the trees they are in their element. Away from them, they will be vulnerable and the advantage will be with us. We know there are not many elves left—the spy Nerith confessed it. We outnumber them a hundred to one, and I will not allow them to trap us with their magic. Hopefully, by then Lyell will have disposed of Lord Brinu Skytree, and they will be leaderless and confused. Either way, they will die. What do you say?'

Timur brought his fist down on the table. 'We will do this!'

'We will!' said Agafya. 'Silverwood will burn, and the elves will burn with it. I will see the Skytree wreathed in flame and the elves dead at my feet.'

'Then so be it,' the Chancellor said grimly. 'Everything is prepared. General, are the troops ready to march?'

'Yes, sir,' he answered. 'We will be ready to set out tomorrow.'

'Then we will,' said the Chancellor.

Days passed in Silverwood and, in spite of everything, they were blissful ones. Lyell was allowed to return to his old home and he spent much of his time there, resting and recuperating. The other elves were more than happy to take care of him, bringing him food and gifts, all their hostility completely forgotten. With the healing of the Skytree, he had become a hero.

Lyell didn't want the attention. He had always had a solitary nature, and after so long away from home he had become even more so. And besides, the last thing he wanted was to be praised and fawned over, least of all by other elves. It sickened him to see them smile and hear them say how he had redeemed himself. The last time he was here they had been all too ready to torture and kill him, but now they seemed to think all that was forgotten.

But it wasn't, not to Lyell. And beneath their smiles they were no different than they had been before, still lost in their delusions. And they *were* delusions—he knew that now, without the slightest doubt. All this murder had accomplished nothing. Of course, he knew better than to say so. It was always possible that they would change their minds about killing him after all, and he needed to maintain the trust he had won back from them. It had come at far too high a cost to risk losing it again.

The leaves that had sprouted on his arms and back stayed lush and healthy, covering him like a living tunic. He considered withdrawing them into his body again, or simply pulling them off, but decided to keep them for the time being, since the others looked at them with such awe. He went without his tunic instead, leaving the leaves on full display, and when he looked at his reflection in the river he had to admit that it looked attractive as well as strange.

He visited the Skytree every day, happy just to see it in full health again, but also because he couldn't shake off the fear that this wouldn't last.

All seemed well enough, however. The leaves stayed green, the bark thick and strong. The children played around it, and the adults came to lounge among the roots and talk about the glory to come. When Lyell came they would call his name, and the children flocked around him, eager to see him.

Lyell said very little on those visits. He channelled more of his magic into the tree, just to be on the safe side, though it was showing no sign of ill-health. Other elves had asked him to visit and restore other, lesser trees, and he had done just that. There was plenty of joy to be had there.

By the end of the week he was feeling much better. The wounds on his side had healed cleanly enough, and he had regained some of the weight he'd lost during his exile. The burn in his lungs was gone now, and he felt stronger and healthier, cleansed by proper food, water, and air. He had even found his belongings, left abandoned in the forest, though he didn't own much. The sprout of the Blackfletch tree was still in its pot, long dead by now, and he buried its shrivelled remains beside the charred stump of its parent tree. That was the only time he returned to the site of his old family tree. He did not want to see that place again, where the remains of the trunk lay shattered and burned. Thick strands of his hair were still embedded in it.

The next day he went back to the Skytree again and saw something that made him pause.

For once there were no other elves there, other than Brinu. But with him was something big and shaggy and pitch-black. It was almost as tall as an elf, broad-chested with hunched shoulders and big, clawed paws. It was growling softly.

Brinu saw Lyell and waved him over. 'Lyell, come.'

He joined them, looking cautiously at the kobold. 'Hello, Ferlak. You've grown.'

The kobold snuffled at him, sniffing his face with his great wet nose. 'Ferlak big kobold now,' he growled. 'You elf, you Lyell?'

'Yes, that is me,' said Lyell.

Ferlak made a rumbling noise in his chest and clumsily petted Lyell's head. 'Ferlak like elf!'

Lyell managed not to fall over. 'So you are about to go out on your quest?' he asked, rubbing his head.

'Yes, I go now,' said Ferlak. 'I go fight humans. Other kobold gather at Bluedell. We hide in trees, fight them there.'

Lyell forced a smile. 'Be brave, Ferlak.'

'Ferlak be brave,' the kobold promised.

'Very good,' Brinu said indulgently. 'Go now, Ferlak. Fight hard for us.'

'Will!' Ferlak rubbed his nose against Brinu's forehead and stomped away, tail waving.

Lyell and Brinu watched him go.

'So the humans are on the march,' Lyell murmured.

'Yes,' said Brinu. 'But have no fear—the kobolds will dispose of them.'

'Yes, the beasts are savage fighters, and Ferlak will serve us well,' said Lyell. His fingers itched for his dagger.

Brinu paused, looking at him. 'You surprise me, Lyell.'

Lyell cocked his head. 'Yes?'

'Yes. You showed such terrible cowardice by abandoning your sacred task, and yet you showed such courage in returning to us. You said that you had turned your back on your own people, yet risked your very life to come back here and save the Skytree.'

'I knew the danger, but I also knew I must redeem myself,' said Lyell, thinking this was at least partly true. 'After what the humans did to me, I knew they were truly our enemies. I made a mistake, but I am still an elf, and the Skytree is everything to me. If need be, I would lay down my life for it.'

'Still, you do not seem angry,' Brinu remarked. 'You came so close to death at our hands.'

Rage burned behind Lyell's eyes, but he gave nothing away. 'It was my just punishment,' he said. 'I accept that. And besides, look at what great good came from it.' He gestured toward the Skytree.

'Indeed,' said Brinu. 'And perhaps it was meant to be this way. You are stronger than you seem, Lyell Blackfletch.'

Lyell risked a quick glance over his shoulder. The clearing was still deserted. *Now*, he thought. *Now is the time...*

'Lyell!' The voice came from behind Brinu, from the tree, and both elves turned in surprise as something small and dark came bursting out from the hole beneath its roots.

'Vender!' Lyell exclaimed.

Tail flitted up into the sky, spitting a fireball, and Vender shouted from his back. 'Lyell, you have to run! Get away or they'll kill you!'

Brinu stared at her in bewilderment. 'What?'

Lyell did not stop to think. With one quick movement, he drew his dagger and thrust it into the older elf's back, slipping it between his ribs with practised ease. Brinu fell with a cry, and Lyell went after him, teeth bared as he struck again and again.

Tail landed on a root, and Vender watched with a horrified expression. 'Lyell! Lyell, stop!'

Lyell did not hear her, and nor did he stop. He struck on until Brinu was dead and then got to work on his body. Once he was finished, he wrenched the head free. Holding it by the hair, he looked up at Vender. 'Come,' he growled. 'We must get out of here.'

He ran.

19

LANDING

Tail clung onto Leaf's back as the deer bounded away through the trees, and Vender hung on beside him, clumps of thick fur wound around her hands. It was brown, tinged with green, and encrusted with grey lichen, and to her it was as thick and strong as rope.

Heart pounding, she looked up at Lyell. The elf sat poised on the saddle, his shoulders pushed forward. Leaves were growing out of his back, all the way down his spine, and there were more on his shoulders and upper arms, and his chest. It was as if he had turned into an elf-shaped tree.

There was blood on his hands. Vender tried not to look at that, but she couldn't stop thinking about what he had done. He had killed Brinu, right there in front of her, and he had looked so *calm* while he was doing it. Now the other elf's head was hanging from the saddle, by Lyell's leg, bouncing horribly every time the deer's hooves hit the ground. Vender tried not to look at that too.

Leaf kept going, following the river through the trees. Vender kept looking back, but she didn't see anyone coming after them, and as they reached the edge of Silverwood, the deer finally slowed down.

Lyell twisted to look back at Vender. 'Vender, are you hurt?' He didn't sound any different, though he looked different.

Vender shook her head. 'Are *you* hurt? Why... why do you have leaves all over you?'

'I told you that the tree was inside me,' said Lyell. 'Now it has put out its leaves.' He was as even as always.

'Oh,' said Vender. 'It doesn't hurt, does it?'

'No. I would shed them, but I left my tunic behind. Vender, what happened to you? How did you come to be under the Skytree? That place is forbidden. None but the Skytrees are allowed to go there.'

'Oh,' Vender said again. She relaxed her grip on Leaf's fur and gently petted Tail. The salamander blinked serenely at her. 'I didn't mean to go there, but there was a tunnel under the Worldroot, so we followed it and... Lyell, there's something down there. Something magic. I—'

Lyell held up a hand. 'Tell me later. For now there is something more important to be done. Will you carry a message for me?'

'Sure I will,' said Vender. 'Where? What message?'

'The humans are coming,' said Lyell. 'The dwarves are with them. They mean to attack Silverwood.'

Vender gasped. 'Oh no!'

'Yes, they asked me to go back there and kill Lord Brinu,' said Lyell, still outwardly unflustered. 'Fly to them, Vender. Find General Lacolo and Agafya. Tell them Brinu is dead and I am bringing them his head as proof. And tell them the kobolds are gathering to ambush them at Bluedell.'

'I will,' said Vender.

'And...' Lyell paused. 'Tell Agafya I am coming back to her, and that I will keep my promise.'

'I'll tell her that,' said Vender. She turned to check on Tail. His wound had healed and the flying membrane on his tail was back in one piece. She patted his snout. *'Fly? Fly now?'*

Tail spread his wings. *'Fly,'* he said eagerly. *'Fly now!'*

Vender pulled down her dragonfly wing eye shield and climbed onto Tail's back. 'We'll find them, Lyell,' she promised.

Lyell smiled at her. 'Thank you. You have been a good friend to me, Vender.'

'You've been good to me, too,' said Vender. 'I really like you a lot, Lyell. You're nice. I'll see you at Bluedell!' she added as Tail reared up off his perch. The salamander took to the air with a clumsy beat of his wings, and then they were off, leaving Lyell to watch them go with that same sadness that had been in him from the moment they first met and had never left. If anything, it had grown even deeper than before.

After so much time underground, Vender enjoyed being in the air again. It was good to feel the wind in her hair and on her face, and the flex and twist of Tail's long body as his wings flicked up and down, the thin bones moving in a rippling motion with the membrane flexing between them.

Everything below looked small again, and as they rose higher, the clouds enveloped them. The air up here was thin, but Vender didn't mind. She trailed a hand in the misty vapour around them, seeing how the droplets gathered on her skin, and laughed aloud.

'Water! The clouds are made of water!'

Tail breathed a stream of fire, and the cloud in front of

them boiled away. Fat drops of rain fell below them, and Vender laughed again. It was enough to let her forget what might happen next, for a little while.

After a while, Tail flew lower, and Vender spotted them below. There, by the river: an endless line of tiny figures, marching along like ants. She tugged on the harness. *'Down! Fly down!'*

Tail obeyed. He swooped straight toward them, pulling his wings back and pointing his head forward like an arrow. Vender lay flat, not wanting to slow him down, her chin pressed against the salamander's neck. The dragonfly wing rattled in the wind, hitting her in the nose, but she could see clearly enough through the net of black veins, and what she saw made her stomach turn. This couldn't be real.

But it was. As they came closer, she saw them more clearly: humans. Thousands upon thousands of humans. Some were on foot, and some were riding huge four-legged creatures that looked as if they were made out of metal. They covered the road by the river, and at the front, leading them, were the dwarves—five of them, riding giant lizards just like Agafya.

Tail made straight for them without needing to be told, possibly because he knew dwarves and saurians far better than he knew humans. He flitted over the dwarves' heads, and Vender looked at them with surprise. They were all the same dark brown colour as Agafya, and the whites of their eyes were silver like hers. They were armoured and carrying weapons, and Agafya was with them.

'More dwarves!' Vender said aloud. 'They aren't all dead!'

Agafya looked up at the sound of her voice and her eyes widened. 'Vender!'

At Vender's urging, Tail landed on the head of Agafya's

saurian. Vender jumped off his back, grinning. 'Agafya, hello! You found other dwarves!'

Agafya smiled back. 'By the gods, you live!'

'I got sick, but Lyell looked after me until I was better,' said Vender.

The other dwarves were looking at her with interest. 'Is that being her, then?' said one of the men. 'The gnome who brought the humans the cure? Lyell's little pet?'

Vender scowled. 'I'm not his pet. I'm his friend. And I'm Agafya's friend too. My name's Vender, and this is Tail. He's from Fivrath, like you.'

'A gnome that rides a salamander. What a sight to see!' said another dwarf.

'I'm the only one who does,' Vender said proudly. 'But Agafya, there's something I got to tell you.'

Agafya glanced at her fellows. She looked amused, and so did they. 'What is it, Vender?'

'Lyell sent me,' said Vender, and their smiles vanished immediately. 'He gave me a message for you.'

Agafya tensed. 'What message? Where is he?'

'He's coming here,' said Vender. 'He's...' She grimaced. 'He killed Lord Brinu and he's got his head. He's bringing it to you.'

'Hah!' a dwarf man with grey hair growled. 'So Brinu is dead. Praise gods! The elf kept his word.'

'Yes, he said you asked him to do it,' said Vender. 'I saw it. But Lyell says the kobolds are going to fight you at Bluedell, where I'm from. They're going to hide in the trees and get you. I had to tell you that.'

Agafya muttered, 'Did he say how many?'

'No, but I think there's going to be lots of them,' said Vender. 'He said I had to tell you, and the human general.'

'Good,' said Agafya. 'Thank you, Vender—you did well.

We must be speaking with the General at once. Vender, will you be going to him and give him your message? He is there.' She pointed out a strong-looking human who was riding not far away on his strange steed.

'Yes I will,' said Vender. 'But Lyell said something else. He's coming here, to meet you. He said he was going to keep his promise.' She paused. 'What did he promise you, Agafya?'

Silence fell. One or two of the other dwarves looked uncomfortable.

'That I would have justice from him,' Agafya said at last. 'Go to the General, Vender. This should not be waiting.'

'Well, you know Lyell is doing the right thing now,' Vender said blithely. 'He's helping you.'

Agafya's mouth grew thin. 'Go, Vender,' she said. 'Now.'

Vender passed on her message to the human general, and after that she and Tail stayed with the army, sometimes riding on one of the human steeds, and sometimes flitting about to investigate the rest of the army or the surrounding countryside. Some of the humans recognised Vender, and others knew her name, and they were all happy to see her. She asked them questions about everything—their names, what were the creatures they were riding, how long it would take to get to Bluedell.

'I'm from there, you know,' she told several people. 'I'm of Bluedell. I never meant to go back, though. There's too much to see outside! Anyway,' she added to the General, 'I've got friends who aren't from Bluedell, and I want to stay with them.'

The General—Paolo was his name—gave Vender an odd look. 'You truly are a strange gnome, Vender.'

'Everyone keeps saying that,' said Vender, though she wasn't annoyed. Maybe she was used to hearing it by now.

Paolo bit his lip. 'Vender...'

'Yes?'

'Vender,' he said again. 'I—no, never mind. It's nothing.'

'All right,' said Vender, though she was puzzled. Some of the other humans had looked as if they wanted to say something to her, but they hadn't. It was as if they were keeping some kind of secret, and it was starting to bother her.

Something else that bothered her was the dwarves. She desperately wanted to talk to them more, but they wouldn't talk to her. Not properly, anyway. She asked about their home in Fivrath, and where they had been all this time, but none of them would say much about it. Their eyes turned hard and their voices went distant. It reminded her of Lyell, and she finally said so. When that happened, Agafya suddenly got angry and told her to go away.

Vender left, hurt and disappointed.

'Why are they being like that?' she wondered aloud to Tail. 'Did I do something wrong? I thought Agafya was nice, but she's so angry all the time. I know she's angry with Lyell, but why is she angry with me? And what are the humans keeping a secret?' She sighed—none of it made any sense. She wished Lyell was there.

That night the humans stopped to camp at Como, and Vender watched with interest while they set up their tents. The more important humans took houses for themselves—the village seemed to be empty. Puzzled, Vender went to investigate. She soon found Figaro's house, but it was deserted.

She sat on the windowsill, legs dangling. 'Where did everybody go?'

'Vender?' a voice called out to her. 'Vender, is that really you?'

Vender looked up and her face split into a smile. 'Figaro!'

The human looked different now. He was wearing armour like the other humans, and there was a rifle slung on his back. 'Vender!' he said again. 'Thank the Pantheon, you're alive.'

'And you're alive too,' Vender said happily. 'Are you a soldier now?'

'Yes, the Chancellor ordered everyone to leave Como and go back to Vaporcitta,' said Figaro. He unlocked the door to his home. 'The other men and I were all drafted into the army. But at least I can spend one last night in my house before I go into battle. Come on, come in!'

He opened the window and Tail and Vender climbed through it. Inside Figaro was busy lighting a fire and opening the other windows—it was a warm night. Other soldiers soon arrived on the doorstep and he let them in.

'There isn't much room,' he told them. 'But you're welcome to use the floor.'

Soon enough the house was crowded with humans, all talking at once. Figaro made some food for them, and they ate and chatted, their helmets left neatly lined up by the door. Vender and Tail found a seat up on a shelf by the stove, and Figaro passed them some food. Vender ate and listened to the humans talk.

'I still can't believe it,' one man said. 'The elves—our enemies, all this time. All my life I was told about them, how wise and powerful they are. My mother even said they were immortal. The oldest race in Hylah. I thought we were so lucky that they chose to help us.'

'You weren't the only one,' said someone else. 'They had us all fooled. But what they've done...'

Vender listened unhappily. She had liked the elves she had met. They'd been so kind to her and it was still hard to accept that they had wanted to kill her. It still made no sense that someone could be kind and cruel at the same time. Why couldn't people just tell the truth about what they were and what they wanted? She didn't think she would ever know.

'Even the gnomes,' someone said suddenly. 'I mean, I still can't understand it. They're the most harmless race in Hylah, but—'

Figaro gestured urgently at the man and a sudden silence fell. All of them turned to look at Vender.

She put her food aside. 'They tried to kill us,' she said. 'They made me sick so I would make the others sick. But Lyell warned me, so I didn't go back. I stayed with him until I was better.' She paused. 'How do you know about that?'

More silence. The humans exchanged glances.

'We should tell her,' one said at last. 'It's not right to keep it to ourselves.'

Vender frowned. 'Tell me what?'

Figaro stood up and came over to the shelf. 'Vender,' he said. 'This is... I'm sorry, but the gnomes are dying. The elves sent plagues to Bluedell and Vaporcitta. They used your brother Bramble in Bluedell. Your family, they...'

Vender looked blankly at him. 'What?'

'Your family are all dead,' said Figaro. 'Some of our men found Bramble still alive and they took him back to Vaporcitta, but he died. The sickness left him, but afterward he let himself waste away and die.'

Vender couldn't seem to hear him properly. 'What?' she said again. It was the only word she seemed to remember just now.

'They're searching for a cure in Vaporcitta,' said Figaro.

'But so far, nothing. At least there's no elvish spy there to stop them this time,' he added bitterly.

Vender sat down with a thump. 'They... they died? My father, my sisters? My brother? But the tribe, they... they were strong. They lived underground, with the Deep Spirit to protect them. They couldn't just...'

'I'm sorry, but it's true,' said Figaro. 'I saw it for myself, in the city. The gnomes were dying everywhere and nothing seemed to help. It's the same as it was for us.'

Vender pulled her hat off and twisted it between her hands, not caring when the dragonfly wing buckled. 'It makes me no sense,' she mumbled to herself. 'It makes me no sense. How...?'

The humans were all looking at her with terrible pity. Figaro hesitated and then gently patted her on the shoulder with his fingertip. 'If it helps you at all, I know how you feel,' he said. 'My whole family died from the plague, here in Como before you came. You saved us, Vender, and you deserve better than this.'

Vender looked down at him. 'The elves, they did this,' she said. 'They went and killed us. Why?'

'Because they're evil,' one man said in a flat voice.

Vender looked at him, then at Figaro, then at her hands. They were gripping her hat so tightly that the knuckles had gone white. 'Lyell's not evil,' she said vaguely. 'Lyell's my friend.'

'That bastard,' someone spat. 'They should have put his head up on the city walls next to the other one.'

Vender didn't hear him. She shuffled over to Tail, putting her back against the salamander's flank, and for once she couldn't think of anything to say.

20

THE AXE FALLS

Lyell reached Bluedell, and soon enough he saw them, and they saw him. Kobolds, hundreds of them. They lurked among the trees where Vender's family had once lived, some of them emerging to glare suspiciously at the elf.

Lyell brought Leaf to a halt and called out to them. 'Ferlak. Is Ferlak here? I need to speak with him.'

The kobolds growled and showed their claws and fangs. A female lumbered over to him, her nostrils flaring as she sniffed at the nervous Leaf. A growl rumbled in her muscular chest. 'What is elf here for?' the kobold demanded, speaking crude elvish.

'I came to bring a message for Ferlak,' said Lyell. 'Is he here?'

The kobolds glanced around, their ears flattening. Finally, the female answered. 'Ferlak is here. Is leader.'

'Can you bring him to see me?' Lyell asked.

After a short pause, the kobold lifted her head and howled. Others joined her, making a horrible rasping, snarling sound. A shiver ran down Lyell's spine.

Still, it worked. There was a rustling from the under-growth, and Ferlak emerged. It was difficult to tell kobolds apart, but Lyell knew him by his bright yellow eyes and his size. By now the kobold had grown to be a head taller than most of his fellows, and his shaggy hide was bloodstained in several places. He saw Lyell and came bounding over to him. 'Lyell!'

Lyell dismounted. 'Ferlak, hello.'

Ferlak's paws were as big as Lyell's face, the claws sharp as daggers, but now, as before, he patted Lyell on the head. 'Friend elf,' he rumbled.

Lyell gingerly patted him in return; the beast stank of rotting meat. 'Ferlak, I have something to tell you,' he said. 'Listen carefully.'

Ferlak's ears tilted forward. 'What you say, Lyell?'

Lyell had hidden Brinu's head in a bag he had made during the journey here, but he cast a quick glance at it anyway. 'I have a message from Lord Skytree,' he said.

'He tell me, we fight here. Kill the humans,' said Ferlak.

'Yes, but he changed his mind,' said Lyell. 'He doesn't want you to fight anymore. You should go, Ferlak. Take the others and find a new home for yourselves.'

The kobolds started to growl again, showing their fangs.

'We fight!' Ferlak insisted.

'This isn't your war, Ferlak,' said Lyell. 'Brinu doesn't want you to fight. He wants you to go away.'

'He not say that!' said Ferlak. 'Humans must die!' Around them the others muttered agreement.

'He did say that,' said Lyell. 'Go, Ferlak. Leave Bluedell.'

Ferlak hesitated and then bared his teeth. 'No. We fight.'

More kobolds had emerged now, and they too were

showing their teeth, their lips curling. They flexed their claws and their tails twitched angrily.

Lyell knew that if he argued any further, he could well be attacked, but he had been prepared for this. 'Very well then,' he said quickly. 'But I must tell you this—the humans know where you are, and that you plan to ambush them here. They are coming this way, along the river. You should fight them in the open, where there is more room.'

'No,' Ferlak said stubbornly. 'We stay here, fight here. Brinu ordered it.'

Lyell finally gave up. 'Do as you wish, then. I must be on my way.'

The kobolds did not try to stop him. He climbed onto Leaf's back and looked down at Ferlak. 'Good luck, Ferlak,' he said and rode off.

After that there was nothing more he could do. He kept following the river. Soon enough he would meet up with the human army, and that would be the end of it. But he wished it didn't have to be this way.

Still, what did it matter what he wished for? He had played his part. What happened next was out of his hands. And at least he would keep his promise to Agafya.

Agafya... Even now the thought of her was enough to put a weak smile on his face. It was foolish, he knew, clinging onto his love for her even though she no longer loved him. What had been between them was gone. But what else did he have to cling to? He recognised his delusion, but did not put it aside. It was all he had left.

He found them at Como, where they were busy breaking

camp. Lyell rode in among the tents and the houses of the village, aware of all the glares being thrown his way. At least this time nobody threw rocks at him. Lyell dismounted and faced the nearest human. 'Tell me where to find General Lacolo,' he said stiffly. 'I am Lyell Blackfletch.'

The human spat at his feet. 'That way, elf. In the village square.'

'Thank you,' Lyell said as stiffly as before. He walked in that direction, Leaf padding after him.

The General was alerted well before Lyell arrived. He was there in the village square as promised, standing by the well. Agafya and the other dwarves were with him.

So was Vender. The gnome was standing on top of the well's little roof, with Tail beside her. 'Lyell!' she called, waving to him.

Lyell smiled briefly at her, then turned his attention to the General. Avoiding Agafya's eye, he opened his bag and pulled out Brinu's head. He hurled it down at their feet. 'As promised,' he said roughly. 'The head of Brinu Skytree. I killed him away from witnesses and made it look like a kobold attack. Perhaps it will fool them, perhaps not. Either way, he is dead.'

The General gave the head a kick. 'Well done,' he said. 'You kept your promise.' He paused. 'And did you warn your people we were coming?'

'Yes,' Lyell told him without hesitation. 'I am sorry, but my people deserve the chance to defend themselves and protect their children. But I also spoke to the kobolds,' he added. 'I tried to fool them into leaving the way clear for you. I failed, but I urged them to abandon their ambush and attack you in the open—they will be more vulnerable away from cover. They may choose to follow my suggestion. I did my best.'

'Thank you,' said the General. 'Can you tell us how many kobolds there are?'

'At least a thousand,' said Lyell. 'You have them out-numbered. Kobolds do not understand strategy. They fight as animals do. They have won in the past by attacking at night and catching their victims by surprise.'

'And they are sent to attack unarmed villagers,' Vitya spat.

'Yes...' Lyell sighed. 'My people have relied upon lies and trickery so far. They don't have the strength or the numbers to attack any other way. But now that time has come to an end.'

'Yes, thanks to you,' said the General.

Lyell finally looked at Agafya. The dwarf's silver eyes were full of hate. 'Is there anything more I can do?' he asked. 'Any other service I can perform for you?'

The human paused. 'Now, nothing. For the time being you will stay with us, as our prisoner. Perhaps in the future—'

'No.' Agafya pushed forward. 'We will not be keeping him. He has served his purpose. Now, I will have my revenge on him.'

'Agafya—' the General began.

Lyell ignored the man's protest. He looked sadly at Agafya and then kneeled before her and lowered his head, baring the back of his neck. 'So be it,' he said.

Agafya stood there for a moment, breathing hard through her nose, and then raised her axe, intoning something in dwarvish. Lyell did not flinch. He waited in silence, eyes on the ground.

The General stepped in. 'Stop!' he said. 'Agafya, stop!'

Agafya did not spare the man a glance. She raised her axe over her head, and then—

'No!'

Something brushed past Lyell's neck—he felt the touch of

air. Agafya shouted and stumbled back, and Lyell looked up to see it. Or, rather, her. Vender the gnome was clinging onto the dwarf's arm, trying desperately to pull the axe out of her hand and shouting all the while. no, no! Stop! Leave him alone!'

'No, no, no! Stop! Leave him alone!'

Lyell stood up. 'Vender!'

Agafya recovered from her surprise and easily plucked the gnome off herself, holding her in her free hand. 'You are daring to do this?' she roared, shaking her. 'Even now you defend him?'

Lyell took a step forward. 'Agafya, put her down!'

Agafya looked up furiously at him, but at that moment Tail swooped down on her. Hissing, the salamander landed on her head and began to bite and scratch at her. Agafya dropped her axe and caught hold of him, throwing him aside. Tail recovered himself and leaped for her other hand, trying to free Vender.

'Fool!' the dwarf raged as she kicked Tail away. 'Little fool! You and your stupid questions and your nagging! You trust him? *Him*? I trusted him and look what he has done to me! My people, destroyed. My family, dead! And now your own family is gone, your people dying, and you are being so blind that you look at an elf and call him *friend*?'

Lyell reached out toward her. 'Agafya, stop, let her go! She is only a gnome. She doesn't know any better. Put her down!'

Agafya stopped shaking Vender, but she didn't loosen her grip on the gasping gnome. 'After everything you have done, the gods allowed you to live,' she growled at Lyell. 'Always a second chance comes your way. Why? What god would do nothing to save my people, yet spare *you*?'

Lyell kept his distance. 'I do not know, Agafya,' he said gently. 'But Vender has no part in this. Let her go. Please.'

'Hah,' said Agafya. 'It is her fault you escaped that tree. You should have been left there to die slowly.'

'But if I had been, then none of you would have learned the truth,' said Lyell. 'Perhaps it was meant to be.'

'And the destruction of the dwarves?' said Agafya. 'What that also meant to be?'

'Perhaps,' said Lyell. 'And perhaps it is meant to be that my race is also dying. I have seen much in my time, Agafya; more than you know. I remember a time when all races flourished. Silverwood grew lush and free, and my people lived in peace. There was never any talk of war. But then Karvbac erupted and half of the forest was destroyed. It put poison into the air and under it the trees began to sicken. And the humans began to build their machines, and the air and the water grew tainted. That was when I was a boy. I grew up surrounded by fear and confusion—none of us knew what to do. We were desperate to make things as they had been before, and that was when the Skytrees began to speak of "cleansing" Hylah... and in time I came to believe they were right. But now I do not know what to do. I am lost, Agafya, as you are lost.'

Silence fell.

Slowly, Agafya loosened her grip on Vender. She was staring at Lyell. 'How old are you?' she said. 'Truly?'

'I am nine hundred and seventy-three years old,' said Lyell.

More silence. The dwarves exchanged glances.

'I do not want to see my people destroyed, even if they have brought this on themselves,' said Lyell. 'I have seen too much death and suffering. Still, the choice is yours. Destroy Silverwood if you wish, but it will not bring anyone back to you, any more than killing all of you would have brought back the Skytree.'

Finally, Agafya put Vender down. 'Go,' she said gruffly. 'Leave me, Lyell. Never let me be seeing your face again.'

'No.' The General finally stepped in. 'We can't afford to let him go free.' He waved to a couple of his underlings. 'Take the elf away. Put him in chains. He comes with us.'

Lyell glanced at him. 'Chains won't be necessary, General. I will come with you.'

'Very well then. But you will be under guard. If you try to leave, you will be shot.'

'I understand,' Lyell said briefly.

Vender limped over to him, with Tail at her side. 'We'll stay with you,' she said.

The army marched on, and Lyell went with them, riding on Leaf. He stayed close to the front, closely watched by the soldiers on their mechanical horses, though as promised he made no attempt to escape. He wasn't certain what he could do from here on—he had killed people, but he wasn't a fighter, and had never handled any weapon other than a dagger. But, for better or for worse, he would see this through.

Vender stayed with him, perched on Leaf's head. The gnome wasn't seriously hurt, but Agafya's fingers had clearly left her with sore ribs—she kept rubbing them.

Lyell kept an eye on her. 'I don't understand why you would want to stay with me,' he said. 'You know... what we did to your people. Don't you?'

Vender looked up at him; there was a nasty bruise over her eye. 'I know,' she mumbled. 'The gnomes are dying just like the dwarves. But you didn't do that. You're on our side now.'

'I am not sure whose side I am on,' Lyell said honestly. 'I

helped my people as well as the humans when I went to Silver-wood. I brought the Skytree back to life.' Mentioning that did something to lift his spirits.

Vender grinned at him. 'I saw it! It was so beautiful! But what if it dies again, like the Worldroot?'

'I don't know,' said Lyell. 'It showed no sign of it while I was there, but perhaps since I left... perhaps we will see.'

'Are they really going to burn the forest?' asked Vender.

'I think they will,' Lyell said sadly. 'If they do, then healing the Skytree will all have been for nothing.'

'I hope they don't,' said Vender. 'But Lyell, I got to tell you what I saw.'

'And what did you see?' asked Lyell, mostly to indulge the gnome.

'When I was under the tree, I saw something,' said Vender. 'See, there was a tunnel under the Worldroot, so me and Tail went along it to find the way out. We were in there a long time —days and days.'

'And it led to the cave under the Skytree?' said Lyell, his interest now piqued.

'Yes, but first there was another cave, and it was full of roots,' said Vender. 'Really big ones, but some of them were smaller. They were all tangled together into a ball bigger than Leaf.'

Lyell frowned. 'A knot of roots?'

Vender nodded. 'And there was magic in them. They were all wrapped around something that glowed like fire, except it was green. One of the roots went to the Skytree —I know that because we followed it and it took us there.'

Lyell breathed in sharply. 'The legend is true! The great trees *are* connected. Did you truly see this, Vender?' He asked the question half hopefully, though he knew it was a pointless one. Vender didn't know how to lie.

'I truly did,' said Vender. 'There were bones there. I think they were elf bones. And there were books too, like the ones Fiorella had. And then Brinu came.'

Lyell's forehead furrowed. 'Brinu? He knew about it?'

'He must have. He went right to the roots and started *doing* something to them,' said Vender. 'Putting his hands on them like you did when you fixed the tree. And then he left.'

Lyell fell silent. He scratched at his chest, making the leaves rustle, and let the implications sink in. This could change everything.

'What do you think it means?' Vender interrupted.

Lyell glanced up at her. 'I think that Brinu may have been trying to save the trees. But his magic was not strong enough.'

'But yours could be,' the gnome said at once.

'Yes,' said Lyell. 'Yes, it could be.'

21

FIRESTORM

They reached Bluedell, and the army came to a halt by the ruins of Fiorella's house. There they formed up—ranks of mounted soldiers, all armed with rifles. The pistolmen stood at the front, dwarfed by the mechanical horses behind them, and the dwarves were there with them. As a non-fighter, Lyell stayed at the back with Vender. The gnome was looking sadly at the ruined cottage, though she said nothing.

'Stay close to me,' Lyell told her. 'I will try to protect you. But if we are cornered, then you and Tail can fly out of reach.'

Vender nodded, still saying nothing. While he waited, Lyell considered what to do. The kobolds might not attack him, since he was an elf, but if they did, he would be all but defenceless. He had only escaped them before by luck. In any case he was still bare-chested other than the coat of leaves, and the humans had no armour that would fit him.

But perhaps his new power could help.

With nothing else to do while he waited for the humans to begin moving, Lyell focused on the energy of the tree inside himself. The wood was there, woven in with his flesh and bone —could he bring it to the surface?

After some consideration, he decided to try it.

The wood responded at once. He breathed in sharply as it started to move inside him, pulling away from his innards and into his skin. It felt as if he were being stuffed full of splinters. But it worked. In moments his skin had grown hard, the wood-grain patterns on them bolder. He raised an arm—it felt stiff, but it would still move—and tapped himself on the chest. His skin wasn't completely rigid, but it felt thick and smooth, exactly like polished wood. Curious, Lyell drew his dagger and scraped it over himself. It left a white line behind, but it didn't hurt and didn't draw any blood.

Satisfied, he put the dagger away. This should give him some protection.

Meanwhile, at the front of the army movement had begun. There was no sign of any kobolds so far, but Lyell knew they must still be here, lying in wait.

The humans obviously knew it too. Agafya and the other dwarves rode away from the army toward the edge of the trees. The saurians lumbered along, shoulder to shoulder, and when they were close they split up, moving along the treeline and then circling around the grove. Soon they were out of sight.

'What are they doing?' asked Vender.

'Burning the trees,' said Lyell.

Sure enough, a short while later he saw smoke beginning to rise from the canopy. Flames followed, glowing orange in the distance, and Lyell heard the kobolds begin to howl.

'They are coming,' he said in a low voice. 'Be ready, Vender.'

Vender drew her tiny bone knife. 'I'm ready.'

Crashing came from between the trees and the undergrowth began to move. The howls grew louder. The first of the kobolds came bursting out into the open, snarling, and hundreds of others followed. They did not hesitate, but charged at the humans at full-tilt, heads down, jaws wide open. Vender screamed, but an instant later the sound was drowned out as the humans began to fight. Pistols fired in a perfectly timed volley, and behind the pistolmen the mounted troops fired their rifles. Dozens of kobolds stumbled and fell, and more scrambled over their bodies to continue the charge. They hit the first row of soldiers with a deafening crash of metal and a chorus of shouts, screams, and snarling roars.

The humans were ready for that. At a shouted command, the horses charged forward, leaping over the line of pistolmen and thundering in among the kobolds. Spinning blades shot out from their flanks and lower legs, and any kobold that got in their way fell back, its hide slashed into ribbons.

Behind them, the grove was now well and truly burning. Flames roared between the trunks, destroying the undergrowth and driving the kobolds before them. And behind that came the dwarves. The five saurians charged out after them, their massive jaws lashing out at any kobold within reach. On their backs the dwarves fought too, their weapons ablaze, hurling fireballs as they hacked and slashed, bellowing war cries in their own language.

And Lyell watched it all with deep, sickening horror at his wood-filled heart. A forest ablaze.

Vender clutched at Leaf's ear. 'My home,' she said in a small voice. 'They can't...'

Lyell looked miserably at her. 'There is nothing we can do.'

But they got no more opportunity to talk. Ahead of them, a gang of kobolds broke through the human line and rushed at them, snapping and snarling. Leaf reared up, bellowing, and at a shout from Lyell the deer charged away.

But the kobolds were faster than they looked. They came after her, bounding over the ground by the river like a pack of wild dogs. Lyell urged her on, but a kobold managed to round her off, and in a moment they were surrounded. Leaf lashed out with her hooves, catching one of them in the jaw. Another one leaped straight for the deer's neck. The beast latched onto her with its claws, and even as Lyell tried to kick it away it sank its teeth into Leaf's throat. Leaf fell sideways, struggling wildly, hurling Lyell from her back. He hit the ground with a sickening crunch, rolled over, and landed in the river.

For a moment he struggled there, too confused to swim, the water closing over his head. But sheer panic was enough to bring him to his senses and he struck out for the bank.

The kobolds were waiting for him. Leaf was down now, her killer ripping into her flesh, and the others left the deer to her death struggles and waded into the river, their claws reaching for Lyell. He tried to swim away from them, but one of them caught him by the shoulder and they dragged him out and onto the bank where they started to rip into him, biting for his neck.

Lyell's wooden skin flexed but did not break. He felt no pain. Desperate now, he drew his dagger and stabbed back at them, aiming for their eyes and throats. He hit one, and the beast fell back with a whine.

A moment later, Tail appeared. The salamander swooped over the kobolds, Vender on his back, and breathed a stream of fire. The kobolds' fur caught alight and they let go of Lyell and stumbled away, beating at themselves.

Lyell took his chance and ran.

The battle was still going on. While the grove burned on in the background, the humans and the kobolds fought, no longer in neat formations but in a messy struggle, each fighter out for himself. Bodies littered the ground, and the dwarves were in the thick of it, recklessly hurling themselves on their enemies. They and the mechanical horses were causing devastation.

Lyell saw Agafya bellowing fearlessly as she planted her flaming axe in a kobold's skull. But she and the other dwarves had made the mistake of separating, and all were surrounded.

Madly, stupidly, Lyell ran toward them. He dodged the humans and kobolds in his way, Tail flying above him, still spitting fire.

Esfir the saurian had begun to struggle. Kobolds attacked the beast from behind, avoiding her lashing tail, and even as Lyell ran he saw two more drag Agafya from the saddle. Dagger in hand, he hurled himself on them. There was no plan in his head, and no real thought either. He lashed out wildly at them, screaming. Tail joined him, his fire withering kobold fur and blistering the skin beneath. Something hit Lyell side-on, and he staggered but did not fall. Agafya pulled herself up, and without a word she stood back-to-back with Lyell and the two of them fought on. Esfir charged in among the kobolds, killing some and scattering the rest.

Red light flashed before Lyell's eyes. Without thinking, he channelled his magic again, and the wooden armour that covered him suddenly warped and split, sending out sharp spikes. He lashed out with his forearms and the spikes punctured a kobold's hide, sending it howling. His dagger had disappeared, but he didn't care. He punched and kicked, hurling the beasts away with a strength he had never felt before, until finally they stopped coming.

Someone touched his arm. 'Lyell?'

Lyell looked up vaguely. 'Agafya?'

The dwarf was staring at him. 'What is wrong with you?'

He looked down at himself. The leaves had been ripped away from his chest and his arms were jagged with wooden spikes that were now slick with blood. But there were no more kobolds. A dozen of them lay dead around him, one with his dagger still sticking out of its chest. Esfir was nearby, eating one of the carcasses.

Lyell turned to Agafya. 'Are you hurt?'

'No.' Agafya was eyeing him cautiously. 'You did not need to have done that.'

Lyell looked briefly at her and then walked away without a word, stopping to retrieve his dagger. He flexed the power inside himself and the spikes smoothed away, drawn back into his body. His skin grew soft again.

The battle was over.

The surviving kobolds were fleeing east, leaving the humans to regroup. Their captains took command and they began to gather up the dead while the forest burned on. The air was thick with smoke and stiflingly hot. It made Lyell retch.

Vender quietly joined him, hopping down off Tail's back to perch on his shoulder. 'Are you all right, Lyell?'

Lyell coughed. 'This smoke is sickening.'

'I know,' said Vender. 'But you went mad just then. I thought you were going to die. And you grew spikes like a hedgehog!'

'I know,' said Lyell. 'But the battle is done now. The kobolds are finished.'

And now Silverwood was defenceless.

~

After the battle the humans got to work. They gathered up their dead and loaded them onto a steam carriage to be taken back to Vaporcitta for burial. The dead kobolds they simply piled up and set on fire, pouring oil over the shaggy corpses to make certain they would burn. Soon the air was thick with the stench of burning fur and flesh, mingled with the smoke that rose from the trees of Bluedell. Dwarvish fire had utterly confused the forest, and Vender's old home had become a raging inferno. Nobody dared to go near it.

Lyell stood on the bloodstained field, Vender perched on his shoulder, and they watched it in silence. But Lyell could not only see it, he could feel it too. The screams of dying trees echoed in his head and burned in his bones, and it was all he could do not to cry out in return. But something did escape. Two silent tears slowly crawled down his cheeks—the first tears he had shed in centuries.

Vender saw them. 'It's gone,' she said in a dull voice. 'It's all gone.' There were tears on her own face.

'Yes,' Lyell said quietly. 'It is as it was when I was a boy and the volcano erupted. Half of Silverwood burned and hundreds of my people were killed. I remember how the ash rained down, and the sky turned yellow and red. I thought the world was coming to an end. My mother choked to death on the poisoned air, and so did many others.'

Vender clutched at his ear. 'And now they want to do the same to Silverwood. How are we going to stop them?'

The smoke stung Lyell's eyes; the tears had already dried away and no more replaced them. '"We"?' he repeated. 'Why you, Vender? What do you care if my home burns? My people tried to murder you, and our home is not yours.'

'I don't care about that,' Vender sniffled. 'Silverwood is beautiful. And I don't want you to lose your home too, Lyell. What are we going to do?'

'There is nothing we can do,' he said heavily. 'The humans

will not listen to me. I am a traitor and an elf. I and my people will be reviled forever.'

'But—' Vender broke off suddenly, looking to her left. 'Agafya...'

Lyell did not look, though he knew the dwarf was there. He kept his eyes on the burning forest. The trees were bare now, their trunks blackened. The lush undergrowth was gone and deep orange flames covered everything. Ash wafted up into the air.

A hot hand touched him on the arm. 'Lyell.'

Lyell finally looked at her. 'Agafya.' He coughed. 'Your fire has done its work.'

Agafya glanced at him, then turned to watch the flames roar. 'We are making good charcoal here today,' she said with a twisted smile. 'Soon enough Silverwood will be nothing but fire as well. And afterward dust and ashes, and charcoal.'

'I know,' said Lyell. He closed his eyes for a moment. 'I do not want to live to see that happen. By the time this is over I could be the last of my people. You would have done me a service if you had killed me, Agafya.'

'And perhaps you would have been doing us both a service if you had killed me in Fivrath,' she said sadly.

'No.' Lyell looked properly at her. 'No, Agafya. You deserve to live.'

'And yet what am I having to live for?' she asked sharply. 'Truly?'

Tentatively, Lyell put a hand on her shoulder. It was hot and muscular under his fingers, and to his surprise she did not shrug him off. 'I think you will find something to live for,' he said. 'Something better than revenge. Death and destruction bring nothing but misery.'

'He's right,' said Vender, breaking her unusually long

silence. 'My home is all gone now, and my family's gone too, and Fiorella. But I know what I have to do now. I have to stay with you, Lyell, and you, Agafya, because you're my friends. We're all the same, aren't we? We've got no families or homes, we've just got each other.'

Silence fell. Lyell heard the gnome's words, and the naïve certainty in them put pain into his heart. Even now, Vender refused to change. Even now, she insisted on seeing others as if they were as pure and innocent as she was. He searched for something to say in reply, but what *could* he say? Nothing was ever going to change her mind about this—he knew that.

But to his surprise, it was Agafya who spoke first. She reached over to take Lyell's hand and gently pressed it against her chest. 'Come,' she said in a low voice. 'You do not need to be watching this. Come with me.'

Lyell paused. 'Agafya?'

'Come,' she said again.

Lyell followed her, turning his back on the inferno. Together they walked past the heap of burning kobolds. The skin had withered away from most of them and he could see their exposed skulls slowly turning to charcoal, the great round sockets full of fire.

But beyond them, untouched for now, the cottage stood. The surrounding garden had grown wild, the fence broken down, but the little paved path could still be seen, leading to the door. The door itself hung open on a single hinge, swinging gently in the ash-laden breeze, and Agafya led him toward it.

Vender stood up on Lyell's shoulder. 'Fiorella's house,' she mumbled. Tail followed them, waddling along the path at their heels and hissing to himself.

Agafya pushed the door open. The single room beyond was badly damaged. Broken glass littered the floor, and there were bloodstains on the flagstones in the kitchen. Books lay scattered and torn apart.

'Fiorella died here,' Vender said in a low voice. 'The kobolds got her.'

Lyell ducked his head to get through the doorway. 'Brinu must have known she had found the cure,' he said. 'Or that she was trying to make it. But he did not reckon with you, Vender,' he added with a faint smile.

Agafya let go of his hand and swept some debris aside with her boot. 'You should be going, Vender,' she said. 'There are sad memories here for you, and Lyell and I must speak alone.'

For once, Vender didn't argue. 'Can you put me down, Lyell?'

Lyell lifted her off his shoulder and gently put her on the floor. 'You should rest, Vender,' he said. 'You were very brave today.'

The gnome nodded. 'I'm going to see if the mother rat is all right,' she said obscurely, and scuttled off to a corner by a broken window, where she lifted a loose floorboard and climbed through the hole underneath. Tail tried to follow her, but was too big for the hole. He tried anyway and hissed irritably when his wings caught.

Vender's small face appeared, peeking out at him. She made strange noises at him, mimicking the salamander's crude speech, and after a short exchange Tail waddled off through the door and into the garden.

Agafya shoved the door back into place, forcing it into its frame, and blocked it with a broken chair.

Lyell sat down on the bed, its quilt in tatters, and watched the dwarf in silence. His heart fluttered—was this it? Agafya pulled out her axe and Lyell braced himself, but then she put it down, leaning it against the wall by the door, and came to sit next to him.

'Are you going to kill me now?' Lyell asked at last.

Agafya took his hand. 'Lyell,' she said. 'Do not be speaking of killing. Not now. I have seen enough death for a lifetime. What use is more blood on the ground? No.'

'You know my life is yours to take,' said Lyell. 'I promised it to you.'

'I know,' said Agafya. 'But Lyell, tell me why I should be doing that. I have lost my home and my family. Now I have so little left, but I have you, yes? So why should I be killing the only one living who loves me?'

Lyell's heart leaped. 'How can you say that, Agafya? You know I still love you, but—'

'Enough,' she said tersely. 'Vender was right. We are all that we are having left. Soon enough we may be dead. But for now, I am yours, my Lyell.'

Lyell said nothing. With a sudden, desperate motion, he pulled her to him and kissed her. And Agafya kissed him back.

'My Lyell,' she whispered. 'My elf. My love.'

22

DUST AND ASHES

The fire burned itself out by morning, and Lyell and Agafya emerged from the cottage to find that everything had turned black and grey. Blinking in the early light, Lyell padded over the grass, which was now covered in ash. The sky too was grey, and the river. The trees of Bluedell had been reduced to blackened stumps, and the other dwarves were there among them, harvesting the charcoal.

Lyell walked among the dead trees, his feet crunching on the charred wood. The air was still full of ash, and he coughed again—his throat was raw.

Agafya, on the other hand, went ahead and joined her people. Yevgeni passed her a chunk of charcoal. She sat down to eat it, while her fellow dwarves all turned to glare at Lyell. 'So you see what we will make of your forest, elf,' Vitya spat.

Lyell did not reply. He silently walked on, Vender perched on his shoulder. 'Show me where it was,' he told the gnome. 'Your people's home.'

'I'll try,' Vender said unhappily. 'It looks so different now.'

Lyell walked on, quartering the ruins as if he were hunting, and Vender directed him as well as she could. He couldn't see anything in any direction but ash and charcoal, and here and there was a stump still smouldering. Agafya quietly followed him, still crunching on her breakfast, and the sight of her lifted Lyell's heart.

After a while, Vender suddenly tensed. 'Here!' she said. 'It's here! Put me down!'

They had reached a large round clearing, and Lyell put the gnome down on the withered grass. She ran back and forth, Tail scampering after her, clearly searching for something.

Agafya took Lyell's hand. 'Why did you bring her here?'

Lyell glanced at her with a smile—the first real one he had worn in a long time. 'I had an idea.'

Finally, Vender stopped. 'Here,' she said, shovelling some debris aside. Sure enough, there was a hole underneath, larger than a rabbit burrow and sloping gently downward. 'This was our tunnel,' she said. She hesitated and looked up at Lyell and Agafya with a solemn expression. 'I don't want to go down there now.'

'You should not,' Lyell agreed. 'There is nothing down there you need to see. But now, let me see what I can do...'

He let go of Agafya's hand and kneeled, putting his hands to the ground. There was nothing here, no pulse of life. But he summoned up his own and put it forth.

Green shoots spiked out of the earth and grew longer, quivering gently as they thickened and put forth leaves. Flowers burst open and pollen puffed into the air, golden as sunshine. Even the sky seemed to lighten a little. On Lyell's back and shoulders, his own leaves sprouted again.

Finally, the elf straightened up. He smiled at Agafya and Vender. 'There.'

The clearing was full of greenery now. Grass and flowers

grew everywhere, fresh and healthy, hiding the blackened ground from view. And among them were the bluebells, nodding in the breeze.

Vender took it all in with an expression of joyful disbelief. 'The flowers! The bluebells—you brought them back!' She grabbed onto one, rubbing the bloom against her cheek.

Lyell was still smiling. 'What is dead and brown may always grow green once more,' he said. 'That is what they say in Silverwood. In time, Bluedell will return to what it was when you lived here. But this will be the first part to return.'

'Thank you!' said Vender. 'Thank you so much, Lyell.'

Lyell glanced at Agafya. 'This is what my people are meant to do. Not to kill, but to make the forest grow.'

Agafya moved closer to him, pressing herself to his side. 'It is beautiful,' she said simply. 'But we must be going back now. The humans will march again today.'

Some of Lyell's joy left him. 'Yes, we must go. Will you come with us, Vender?'

The gnome looked keenly at them. 'So you love each other again? That's good. I knew you could make up.'

Lyell and Agafya exchanged pained glances. 'Come,' Lyell said at last. 'They will be waiting for us.'

The humans had made camp on the field by the remains of Bluedell, and when Lyell and the others returned, it was to find that a portion of the army had already formed up, standing neatly in ranks, their mechanical horses ticking away. General Lacolo was there with Timur and the other dwarves.

'There you are,' he said as Lyell approached. He eyed

Agafya. 'I thought you might have tried to run, but if she was with you...'

'I would not let him go,' said Agafya. 'Are the men ready, General?'

'Yes, I was about to send some to find you, Agafya.'

'No matter,' she replied. 'I will not be going with them, Paolo.'

The other dwarves looked at her in surprise. 'Why?' said Timur. 'This was our plan.'

'Yes, but you must be going without me,' said Agafya. 'I will be being here to support the humans who are still here. My fire will burn Silverwood from the front.'

Lyell frowned, but he said nothing. Nobody cared what he thought.

'Very well,' said the General. 'You are my ally, not my underling, and perhaps it would be better to have one of you here.'

'Thank you,' said Agafya, ignoring the stares of the other dwarves. 'I will guard the elf for you. If he tries to escape, it will be me who is killing him.'

The General nodded. 'Now, Vender, may I speak with you?'

Vender, now perched on Lyell's shoulder with Tail on the other side, looked up. 'Yes, Paolo?'

'Can you help us?' he asked. 'You and Tail can be messengers, to keep our men in touch. Will you do that for me?'

'Sure,' said Vender. 'Me and Tail can fly back and forth.'

'Thank you.' He smiled. 'You can go with Timur and the other dwarves when they leave and fly back tonight.'

'I will.' Vender clambered around the back of Lyell's neck and climbed onto Tail's back. The salamander flitted down onto the head of Timur's saurian, where he perched with one foot clutching a spike.

'Then everything is ready,' said the General. 'Good luck.'

He turned to his troops and gave a short, sharp command and the mechanical horses stirred into life. Only mounted troops would be going on this mission. They clanked away, the dwarves in the lead, leaving the rest to wave them off with good wishes. Timur, Yevgeni, Vitya, and Irina all looked back at Agafya as they left, and Lyell caught the narrow, suspicious looks on their faces. But Agafya ignored them. She stood proud, stone-faced, and waited until they had gone.

Afterward, she turned to the General again. 'I would like to be requesting to have the cottage,' she said formally. 'The elf can be locked up there, and I will be keeping a close watch on him.'

The General looked suspicious too, but all he said was, 'Very well. We'll be staying here until our strike force is in position. Until then, the cottage is yours.'

'Come, then,' said Agafya. She gave Lyell a rough shove. 'You have seen enough sky, elf.'

Lyell went with her meekly enough, but the moment they were alone in the cottage he turned to her and said, 'Is this true? Tell me it is not true. You didn't ask to stay behind only so—'

Agafya silenced him with her lips.

Days passed, and in a way they were the happiest of Lyell's life, in a way. Agafya stayed by him, as promised, and though it soon became clear that the humans had guessed what they were doing, nobody said anything. They cleaned up the cottage together, and Lyell used his magic to make the garden flourish. Before long it was laden with healthy fruit and vegetables, and the human soldiers eagerly helped themselves. Lyell ate some, and it tasted good—clean and pure. In time, the sky cleared and the air became less stifling. It left him feeling stronger and healthier.

And then there was Agafya. She was there with him, impossibly, and her attentions toward him were as hot and passionate as they had been in Fivrath.

Passionate... and yet desperate. Lyell sensed it every moment they were together. It was there in her voice, in her burning-hot kisses, in her powerful embraces. Every word and glance that passed between them carried a note of desperation, and it was a desperation that Lyell shared.

He knew this couldn't last, just as she must have known. Sooner or later they would be torn apart again, and this time it could well be for good. Once Silverwood was destroyed, the humans might well kill him since he had outlived his usefulness. That or they would send him into exile, or keep him as a slave. Either way, their time together would be over soon enough. For now he took comfort from her, and perhaps he gave it to her in return. He hoped so.

Vender came back from time to time, bringing reports from the strike force. She reported directly to the General, but always visited Lyell and Agafya afterward, and not for the first time Lyell was astonished by the little gnome's resilience.

'We got attacked by elves,' she said on her third visit. 'They came out of the trees and threw spears at us. Timur got hurt, but he's all right. Two of the humans died, though.'

'And are they close now?' asked Agafya.

'Yes,' said Vender. 'I'm going to fly back tomorrow and tell them it's time to start attacking. The General's going to take everyone else to Silverwood in the morning.'

'Then it's over,' said Lyell. 'Or it shall be soon enough.'

'I wish we could stop it, but you said we can't,' said Vender. 'I don't want to help the forest burn, but Paolo asked me to help. I couldn't tell him no.'

'You could have, but it is being too late for that,' said Agafya. 'Go on, Vender—go and rest. We will be seeing you again in Silverwood.'

The gnome nodded sleepily. 'Tail's tired too. I should find food for him.'

She shuffled off with her steed, leaving Lyell and Agafya together by the gas heater, which Figaro and another human had fixed. The warmth of the blue-edged flame was pleasant on Lyell's face, but the sight of it stirred up the dread in his stomach. 'Tomorrow, we march on Silverwood,' he muttered. 'If I were not such a coward, I would make my escape and re-join my people. If I must die, then I may as well die fighting beside them.'

Agafya touched him gently. 'I would have been saying you were not a fighter once, but now I am knowing better. When you fought the kobolds beside me—I have never seen such a thing. You are very powerful now, Lyell.'

'Yes, and perhaps once my people are destroyed the humans will keep me alive for it,' Lyell said bitterly. 'Nothing healthy can grow in that foul city of theirs, but with my magic that could change.'

Agafya paused. 'I never heard you speak that way before,' she said, smiling. 'Once I thought you were a cold man, Lyell— that there was no anger in you. But I am seeing it now. You have a dwarvish ferocity.'

'My people prize the ability to hide our feelings,' Lyell

confessed. 'At least from other races. I was an ambassador for so long, I became a master at showing nothing of what was in my heart or my mind.'

'But there is no need to be doing that with me, Lyell,' she said.

He kissed her. 'No. No need. This is our last night, Agafya... the last. I know it.'

'Then let it be truly ours,' she told him softly.

Lyell held onto her. 'How can you have forgiven me, Agafya?' he asked in a low voice. 'Because of me you lost everything. Even if I had a change of heart, that cannot change what I did. Nothing can.'

A brief look of bitterness showed in Agafya's eyes. 'I am knowing that. And perhaps I have not forgiven you, Lyell. But now we are not so different anymore. My people are gone, and you have lost yours.'

Lyell stared at his hands. 'Yes... yes, I have. I have no people now. Even if I live to see this end, I know I will be alone. My people will be gone, and everywhere I go I will be hated. But I accept that as my punishment. Perhaps death would have been too easy a release.'

'Hush.' Agafya brushed his cheek with her fingers. 'Do not be speaking this way, Lyell. I too was wanting death, after the fall of Fivrath. I felt that it was my fault, what had happened—you know that. But I found a reason to live.'

Lyell smiled weakly. 'And what was that reason?'

Agafya kissed him. 'You. You, my Lyell. You are my reason now.'

'You cannot mean that,' said Lyell.

She took him in her arms, holding him in a hug so fierce it could have crushed his ribs. 'But I do,' she said. 'You are my reason now. You were all I had at the end, and you are all I am having now. Let us forget what has been—let me be your reason. When this is over, we can be together, as you promised we could be. We can be finding a new home and raise our children there, and only the future will matter.'

Lyell's heart swelled. 'Truly?'

'Truly, my sweet one.' Agafya kissed him again.

Lyell kissed her back. 'Then you are my reason,' he said. 'You are.'

The next day came, all too soon, and Lyell and Agafya left their cottage together. The humans were breaking camp and in no time at all they were ready to go. They formed into their neat ranks, horses at the front and steam carriages carrying supplies at the back. With Leaf dead, Lyell had to ride on one of those. The driver gave him the filthy, contemptuous look he was used to by now, but he said nothing, and Lyell sat down on a crate with his long legs dangling. Agafya rode alongside the carriage, mounted on her saurian, and the army moved off.

They marched steadily along the river, the mechanical horses glowing in the morning sun, and by noon they had reached the edge of the forest where the ground sloped upward. The troops came to a halt and immediately got to work. While some of them set up a new camp, others rode their mechanical horses up into the trees. There they activated the blades, which sliced through the trunks around them. Lyell winced at the sound of breaking timber as the trees fell. Agafya went with them, and he saw the flickering of flames as she destroyed the poisonous blooms that lay in wait. He had warned her about those himself, once upon a time.

The humans brought the newly cut lumber back and set to

building a defensive position. While the tree-cutters had been busy, others had used a set of steam shovels to dig trenches and a mound of earth. Now they built wooden frames in front of the trenches, sharpening the ends of each piece of wood into lethal stakes.

Lyell knew there was truly no need to go this far. The humans out-numbered and out-weaponed the elves so badly that there would likely be no real fight at all. But he would see soon enough.

That afternoon, not long after the defences were completed, he saw the smoke. It drifted up into the pale sky in a grey haze, and before long the humans were pointing it out to each other and murmuring. Lyell's fists clenched. It was happening. The moment he had dreaded had come.

As evening drew on, the smoke grew steadily thicker and closer. It would take some time to reach them, but sooner or later it would. Silverwood would be consumed, bit by bit.

The sun went down in a glorious mass of red and gold, and it was a colour that did not leave the sky. Night enveloped the camp, and Lyell saw the glow on the horizon. It was faint, but it was there: the glow of fire. His throat tightened.

This is your fault, his conscience whispered. *You did this.*

Impulsively, he jumped down from the back of the carriage. Where was Agafya?

He wandered through the camp, utterly oblivious to the taunts from the humans. Agafya had not left his side for this long since their time in the cottage, and he needed her now.

He found her by the earth mound, standing among the sentries. A torch stood beside her, burning in a metal holder thrust into the ground. Its light flickered over the dwarf's silver eyes and highlighted the strands of white in her yellow hair.

Lyell quietly joined her and took her hand.

Agafya looked sideways at him and her eyes narrowed. 'Now at last, it begins,' she said in a low voice. 'Silverwood burns.'

Lyell did not let go of her hand, but he said nothing because there was nothing to say. He wondered vaguely where Vender was.

He did not sleep that night, and neither did Agafya. They stayed where they were, both silent, both watching. The fire steadily burned closer, the glow in the sky increasing until the stars themselves were lost among the red haze. The wind was blowing their way, and soon enough it began to carry ash and smoke toward them.

Lyell didn't feel tired; in fact, he felt nothing in particular. His ability to feel anything at all seemed to have gone away somewhere, and he felt lost in a dream of smothering darkness. But Agafya was there, and he stayed close to her. There was some small comfort in that.

A sickly dawn finally came, and the humans stirred. The fire was even more obvious now. Lyell could see its glow among the trees, and the smoke was thicker than ever.

'Forgive me,' he muttered aloud.

As the sun rose higher, Lyell saw movement. He pointed quickly. 'Look, there!'

The humans heard him. The sentries readied their weapons and others hurried to join them. But there was no real need for it. Lyell watched as the other elf staggered into view, bumping into the trees still standing at the edge of the forest. It was a man, and he was unarmed, and well before he reached the defences he fell forward onto the ground. Lyell could hear him moaning.

Agafya was watching too, her eyes narrow. 'And so the first of them dies,' she said.

Lyell moved away from her. 'Agafya...'

She looked at him and sighed. 'Now is your time to be seeing what I saw, Lyell,' she said. 'I cannot feel pity for your race, and I do not. Let them all die.'

Lyell grimaced. 'There must be—'

'No,' Agafya said coldly. 'The time for elves is over. Will you stand with me and watch them die, or...?'

Lyell gave her an agonised look, knowing she knew that he felt now what she had felt in Fivrath that day. As if a dagger was twisting in his heart. And now, as it was then, he could not do nothing.

'I must go,' he whispered. 'Forgive me, my love.'

With that he turned and ran up the dirt mound to the top, shoving humans out of his way. He vaulted over the trench and leaped over the barricade. Shots rang out, and he felt the bullets hit him—but it didn't hurt and he sprinted away, charging headlong toward the burning forest as fast as he could go.

23

THE HEART OF EVERYTHING

Lyell knew he was running to his death, and he didn't care. Other elves ran past him, choking on the smoke-filled air, and behind him he could hear the faint crack of gunfire as the humans gunned others down. The fleeing elves realised what was going on and they faltered, stopping among the trees. But the fire was there, roaring toward them—a great wall of it, consuming the trees. There was nowhere else to go.

Still, Lyell did not hesitate. He ran toward the fire, ready and willing to let it take him.

Someone caught him by the arm. 'Lyell!'

He faltered, looking back, and saw Eala's soot-stained face. The other elf's eyes were red-rimmed and full of terror. She had cut herself on his spikes, but didn't seem to have noticed.

'Eala,' he said blankly.

'Lyell,' she said again. 'Where were you? We thought you were dead. Where are you going?'

Lyell shook her off. 'To my death,' he growled and ran on, hurling himself into the heart of the fire. The flames enveloped him and in an instant his hair had caught alight. His leaves withered, his pants went up, and his wooden skin steamed and split, blood and sap hissing in the heat. Lyell screamed, but he did not stop running, even as he felt the fire consume him. Smoke poured into his lungs. He couldn't breathe, couldn't see. All around him was light and agonising heat, and soon, very soon—

A sudden blast of cold air hit him and he fell down, unable to run any further. Instinctively, he rolled on the ground and the flames that had enveloped him went out. Afterward he lay there, gasping for breath, aware of only one thing: he was alive. The fire had moved on.

He forced his eyes open, but all he could see was blurry blackness. Had he gone blind?

But no, there was light there too. Lyell dragged himself up, pain crackling over his skin. He was in another ruin, surrounded by burned trees. Flames flickered here and there, but the worst of the inferno had passed. He had survived.

Gingerly, he checked himself. His leaves were gone and his wooden skin was blackened. The spikes had burned away. He carefully used his magic and the wood withdrew, leaving untouched skin behind. His hair had burned off, but other than that he was unhurt.

With a groan, Lyell heaved himself to his feet. Everything around him was dead. Death had come to Silverwood, just as it had in Bluedell. He had survived only to see it.

But he was not alone for long. Even as he limped away toward the Skytree's clearing, he heard a great lumbering and crashing as four saurians came charging toward him, with a squad of mounted humans behind them, their blades cutting down the trees in their path.

Lyell hesitated, not knowing whether he should try to escape from them or wait for them to arrive and let them do what they would. Before he could make up his mind, a shout came from above and Tail came swooping toward him. Vender leaped off his back and onto Lyell's shoulder, then hugged him around the neck. 'Lyell, there you are!'

Lyell patted her on the back. 'Vender. I can never get away from you, can I?'

'Never,' said the gnome.

The dwarves were on them a moment later, flaming weapons drawn, but Vender shouted, 'Leave him alone!'

Timur glared briefly at him and then spurred his steed on. The saurian charged by and the others followed. Lyell threw himself flat, narrowly avoiding the spinning blades as the horses followed, Vender still clinging to his neck. None of them stopped to speak with him, and in moments they were gone.

'They nearly killed us!' Vender exclaimed as Lyell got up.

'Yes,' he said, his voice was harsh with smoke. 'But not on purpose. It would seem I mean so little to them now that it was not worth the time to kill me.'

'No!' said Vender. 'They let you go because you're their friend now.'

Lyell groaned internally, but he said nothing and walked off. He made for the Skytree, if only because there didn't seem to be anywhere else to go. Tail followed.

Vender took everything in with a solemn expression. 'They really did it.'

'Yes.' Lyell gritted his teeth. 'My people are being slaughtered now. I saw it. I will be the last of my kind, Vender, if not for very long. The humans will search for me, and I don't know what they will do with me when they find me.'

'They wouldn't kill you,' Vender said with certainty. 'I wouldn't let them anyway.'

Despite himself, Lyell felt a little better knowing she was

there. He patted her again, saying nothing, and went on up to the clearing. The Skytree was there and, just as he had feared, it was dead. Its trunk had turned black and its leaves and branches were still ablaze. Several dead elves lay collapsed among the roots.

'Oh no,' Vender groaned. 'It's dead again.'

'Yes,' said Lyell. 'As I knew it would be. Perhaps it died before the fire even came here.'

Tail perched on a root and Lyell sat down below him, resting his back against the charred wood. Vender climbed up onto the root. 'What are we going to do now, Lyell?'

'I don't know,' he said honestly.

'We could leave,' said Vender. 'Find another forest to live in. Or you could bring this one back to life.'

'I could, perhaps,' said Lyell. 'But with my people dead, who would be here to see it?'

'You would be,' said Vender. 'And me and Tail. You should see that cave I told you about, where the roots are.'

Lyell paused. 'Yes, I should see it for myself. And perhaps my magic could do something.'

'You go,' said Vender. 'I'll stay here and watch out for danger.'

'Very well then.' Lyell got up and smiled at her before he made for the cave where Brinu had lived, whose interior he had never seen and had been forbidden to see. But what did that matter now? Brinu was dead, and there was no one left to object.

The cave entrance had been obscured, covered by a mat of broken branches. Lyell moved to lift it aside. To his surprise he found that the covering wasn't simple wreckage, but had been cunningly woven together into a kind of crude door. He picked it up and leaned it against the tree, and after a moment's consideration he lowered it after him as he went into the cave, hiding the entrance from view. They wouldn't find him down here.

The entrance led to a short tunnel, tall enough for him to stand upright, and the moment Lyell entered he saw the faint flickering of light beyond.

A faint hope began to waver in him and he walked down the tunnel into a large cave. It was lined with wood; the roof was the very base of the Skytree, held up by root pillars and walled by more roots, magically shaped into shelves, chairs, a table, and a simple bed. At the centre of the cave was a deep pool, edged with stone, its blue depths constantly churning and bubbling as water erupted from the earth and poured out through the channel at the back of the cave, rushing through a gate made of roots and away into Hylah. This was the birth-place of the river, and here the waters glowed, throwing their gentle light over everything.

Lyell stood in the entrance, blinking, and they looked back at him in silence. They were there by the pool, rising to meet him, some already saying his name. 'Lyell. Lyell Blackfletch. He's alive!'

A painful smile tugged at the corners of Lyell's mouth. 'Hello,' he said, speaking elvish.

They rushed over to him, and in a moment he was surrounded. The children of his people, every single one of them, were clutching at his hands, saying his name. Some even hugged him.

'You came back. You came back to save us!'

There were adults too, but only a handful of them. Kiya Deertrack was there, and Ardrathar Rocktree, and a few others, all of them parents. They looked at Lyell with wonder and amazement.

For the first time in years, he laughed—real, light, happy laughter. He hugged the children back fiercely. 'We are not dead,' he said. 'Not all of us.'

'The hero!' one of the children said happily. 'Lyell the hero came back, and he's going to save the forest.'

Lyell looked up and saw that even the adults were looking at him with hopeful expressions, their golden eyes shining. They, too, believed it. He was a hero, their saviour come back to them in their hour of need.

'This is my place,' he said softly. 'This was always my place, here in Silverwood with you. I never should have left.'

Kiya came over to him, touching him on the arm. 'You will save us, won't you?' she asked in a low voice. 'You have the power to save the Skytree.'

Lyell set his jaw. 'I will try,' he promised. 'I think—'

A sudden noise came from above and everyone froze. Great thuddings and grindings shook the earth and loose dirt rained down from the ceiling. Several children began to whimper.

'Stay here,' Lyell whispered. He edged over to the tunnel, looking up toward the entrance and silently thanking the holy spirits of nature that he had thought to cover it up again. He crouched just below it, listening intently. He could hear the clanking of mechanical horses and the lumbering of a saurian and a faint *thunk* of metal on wood.

Lyell bit his tongue. His heart was pounding. If they found him here, if they discovered the tunnel, they would kill him and everyone else. Even the children. He was certain of it.

A voice spoke from above and the sound of it hit Lyell like a physical blow. 'Where is he? Vender, did you see him?'

'*No,*' Lyell breathed. Not Vender. He should never have left her up there.

'Why are you looking for him?' the gnome's small voice piped up. 'You aren't going to kill him, are you?'

'Tell us where he is,' Agafya said impatiently. 'Did you see him?'

Lyell couldn't move. He put his hands over his stubbly head and waited for the inevitable.

'Yes, I saw him,' Vender replied. 'He ran through the fire. The other dwarves were going to kill him, but I told them not to. Then he ran away. He said he was going back to Whitebark, where the Worldroot tree is. I wanted to go with him, but he wouldn't let me.'

The knot of tension loosened in Lyell's stomach and he stared upward in disbelief.

'Whitebark?' someone else said after a while. 'That is a dead place. He won't survive there. In any case, why not let him go? Killing him would be easy. Forcing him to live in the knowledge that his race is dead is a far better punishment, wouldn't you say?'

'I am agreeing with that,' Timur rumbled.

There was a brief silence, and then Agafya spoke again. 'I hope he has survived somewhere, but I am thinking we will not meet again in this life. And perhaps it is being fitting that he must live on in the knowledge that his people are extinct. But for me, I must return to Fivrath.'

After a time, a human voice spoke. 'I think we can go now and join the search. If any elves are left here in the forest, we'll find them and dispose of them.'

'I don't think there are any left,' said Vender.

'I agree, but we should check,' said the human. 'Vender, will you come with us?'

'No,' the gnome answered. 'I'm going to stay here with Tail.'

'Are you sure?' the human asked.

'Yes,' said Vender. 'You go on, Figaro.'

'Will you come and visit us in Como, or in Vaporcitta? You'd always be welcome.'

'I think I might,' Vender said with a smile in her voice. 'Goodbye, Figaro.'

Then they were gone, and Lyell breathed again. He retreated to the cave as quietly as he could. The children were at the far end, by the waterfall, all of them clearly petrified. Kiya had an arrow ready on her bow.

'It's all right,' Lyell told them. 'They left. Vender protected us.'

'The little gnome,' Ardrathar muttered. 'We tried to kill her...'

'Yet she forgave you,' Lyell said sternly. 'If not, we would all be dead now. But stay quiet. We should wait here until we know they are gone.'

And so they waited. There was some food stored in the cave and they shared it out, or rather Lyell did. Everyone seemed to think he was in charge now. He shrugged and saw to it that everyone got an equal share, then lowered himself into the pool and bathed, scrubbing off the soot and ashes and the shrivelled remains of his hair. The water was cool and soothing, its current a caress on his rippled skin, and as he bathed he felt an energy flowing into him. The sap in his blood pulsed faster, the wood in his muscle grew stronger, and his heartbeat felt steadier.

He got out reluctantly, and Kiya passed him a new set of clothes: a tunic shaped like two leaves, bark-patterned pants, and a pair of soft deerskin shoes. He put them on gratefully.

'Tell us what happened to you,' one child urged. Lyell sat down on a chair that one of the adults politely left for him.

'Where were you? We thought bad kobolds carried you away.'

Lyell smiled grimly—so his ploy had worked. 'A kobold killed Brinu. I saw it happen. I chased after the beast, but it led me out of Silverwood,' he invented. 'I was afraid to come back in case you blamed me for what happened to Brinu.'

'Never,' said Ardrathar. 'You are the blessed one who saved the Skytree. But perhaps it is to be expected that you were afraid of what we might do. After all...'

Lyell nodded. 'Yes. Anyway, the humans took me prisoner again—I came across their army. Then...'

The others listened closely as Lyell spoke, mixing in some truth to make it more plausible. He talked about the battle with the kobolds at Bluedell, and how the forest had burned, and then the final battle, when he had made his escape at last. Which, he supposed, he had.

'I no longer cared what happened to me,' he said honestly. 'I threw myself into the fire expecting to die, but my powers protected me. And now I have found you.'

'All the forest burned, didn't it?' said Kiya.

'Yes.'

The others groaned aloud. 'I heard the Skytree dying,' said one of the adults. 'We all heard it. But the rest of the forest...'

'Gone,' said Lyell. The word hurt to say.

'But it will come back,' said Ardrathar. 'You will bring it back, Lyell. I know you will.'

'I will try, as I said,' said Lyell. He had already spotted the curtain at one end of the cave. The others didn't seem to have noticed it, but he could feel the power coming from behind it. He would go down there later once he knew for certain that the humans had left.

Hours passed. The elves stayed where they were, swapping

stories in low voices. Kiya even sang—a low, quiet song of mourning. Though Lyell mourned too, he was glad to know one thing. The fire would have destroyed the plants Brinu had used to create the plagues—the twisted creations with their poisonous spores that so many unwitting visitors had been touched by. All it took was a single spore to infect the victim. But now they were surely gone, and no more would take their place—Lyell would see to it.

While they waited, they sometimes heard movement above. Humans went by on their mechanical steeds, and Lyell heard their voices and the thud of metal hooves. But nobody discovered the tunnel. Several times he overheard Vender repeating her lie about how he had fled to Whitebark.

'That gnome is helping us!' one of the children breathed.

'Yes.' Lyell smiled to himself. 'She's our friend, Kynell. Or she is my friend. In all the time I was trapped among the humans, she was the only true friend I had.' He said it without thinking, but as he did, he realised it was true. It always had been. In all the time he had known her, Vender had never lied to him, nor had she ever condemned him for what he had done. She had been the first to forgive him, and she had never stopped trusting him.

Finally, with the humans long gone and after hours of silence, Lyell risked going to the entrance. He peeked out between the branches, but couldn't see anything. 'Vender!' he hissed. 'Vender, are you there?'

The gnome arrived at once. 'Lyell, are you all right?'

'Yes. The humans—have they gone?'

'Yes,' said Vender. 'I've been waiting to see if they would come back.'

'Will you go and check?' asked Lyell. 'Find out what they are doing?'

'Yes, of course! I'll come back soon and tell you.'

Lyell smiled at her. 'Thank you, Vender.'

Vender paused. 'You smile a lot more now than you did before,' she said. 'I like that.'

She left, and Lyell waited by the entrance. He was still smiling.

A few hours later, Vender returned. 'They're gone!' she called down to him. 'The humans are leaving! I talked to Paolo —he said they're all going home now. He said now that the forest is burned the elves won't have anywhere to hide anyway, so if any of you are still alive you'll just wander away some-where and die. But that won't happen, will it?'

Lyell pushed the cover aside. 'I hope not,' he said. 'Come in, Vender.'

Tail hopped down through the entrance, Vender on his back, and Lyell pulled the cover back down. And then, surprising even himself, he picked up Vender and hugged her.

Vender hugged him back around the arm. 'I'm so happy you're safe!'

'And I am happy to see you too, my little friend,' Lyell said with complete sincerity. 'Now come!' He sat her on his arm and went down the tunnel to where the others were waiting. Vender gasped at the sight of them.

Vender gasped at the sight of them. 'They aren't gone!'

Kiya gave Vender a narrow-eyed look. 'A gnome, here in this sacred place?'

'A gnome belongs underground,' Lyell said firmly. 'Yes, Vender?'

'Sometimes we do,' she conceded. 'But I like to fly. Anyway, it's all right now,' she told the elves. 'The humans are going home. They don't know you're here.'

'You finally learned to lie, Vender,' said Lyell. 'I thought you would tell them where I was.'

'I thought of it, but I didn't want them to hurt you,' said Vender. 'Anyway, are you going to do it now?'

'Do what?' said one of the children.

'Save the forest, of course,' said Vender. 'I told him about the special place I found, where Brinu was.'

Lyell put her down next to Tail. 'Yes,' he said. 'Now is the time.'

He went over to the curtain and pulled it aside. Sure enough, behind it was the entrance to another tunnel. Dug through the earth, its entrance was lined by roots, and one root in particular ran along its wall. And, at the far end, he could see a faint green glow.

Lyell squared his shoulders and set out toward it. The others followed, talking in low voices.

'What is this?' Kiya murmured.

Lyell said nothing. He pushed on to the end of the tunnel, and there it was: a great cave, nearly as large as the one he had left behind. Elvish bones littered the floor. Books sat against one wall. And at the centre of the chamber, hanging at head-height, was the heart of everything. Dozens and dozens of roots, some small, some large, and some massive. Green light pulsated from within them.

Around Lyell, the other elves exclaimed loudly.

'The legend!' Ardrathar cried. 'The legend is true!'

Lyell went over to the knot of roots, which was as big as his poor, faithful deer. 'Yes,' he breathed. 'It is true. Brinu kept it a secret, as his predecessors must have. But we remembered.' He turned to look back at them. 'The legend is true,' he repeated. 'The world is all connected and this is the place where it meets.

The great trees are the true beauty and magic of Hylah, and they are all one, as the land is one.'

Tail landed on one of the roots, away from the knot, and Vender looked down from his back. 'See?' she said. 'I told you it was here.'

'You mean you found this place, Vender?' said Kiya.

'Yes I did,' said Vender. 'I followed the tunnel from under the Worldroot tree. I told Lyell about it. And I think—'

Lyell waved her into silence. 'Wait and see.' He turned back to the knot, took a deep breath, and placed his hands on it. It was time.

The power flowed out of him, lush and green. Sap pounded in his veins, and his leaves began to sprout again. The roots responded, creaking and groaning as their own sap began to flow once more. Those that had been dead, grey, and cracked turned green and grew a fresh coating of bark. At their heart, the glowing light grew steadily brighter and brighter. The flickering died down, and the light became steady. Around Lyell, the other elves began to sing.

Lyell could feel the power leaving him. His heart pattered frantically, his limbs shook, and his vision wavered as it had before. But he didn't care. He kept going, even when the wood in his flesh began to crack and the sap in his blood slowed and dried. His eyesight grew even weaker; the world around him darkened. He closed his eyes, but then they snapped open again, and as he stared into the glow of magic, he saw it—he felt it.

He saw the trees. The great trees. The Skytree, the Worldroot, and others. So many others. There was one in the human city, and one in Fivrath, and others far to the north, the east, and the west. Trees with no names. Trees long dead and forgotten. But now he felt their presence inside him, their ancient strength pressing against his own, demanding his help. And he was there to help them.

He gritted his teeth and gave one last push, and it happened. He saw it happen.

The Skytree's charred bark fell away and it burst back into life, leaves and flowers exploding. Far away, the Worldroot sprouted. In Vaporcitta, the roof of the Pantheon Temple broke apart as massive branches thrust into the sky. In Fivrath, another tree grew in the middle of the city—a strange black, red-leafed tree, its branches spreading over the streets where the dwarves had once lived. And others. Trees of all kinds, all ancient, all filled with the pure power of life. Around them the lesser trees and other plants grew. It happened in a great rush of energy, and Lyell felt it at his heart. He cried out—not a cry of pain, but of ecstasy.

This time, he did not black out. He fell back from the roots, and they were there to catch him. The other elves were still singing. They supported him, crying out his name, and Vender was shouting it too.

Lyell ached all over, but it was a pleasant kind of ache. He looked muzzily at himself and laughed softly when he saw what had happened. The leaves were back, as he had expected, but something else had sprouted too.

Lyell Blackfletch had flowered.

He tried to stand up, but his legs were weak, and he fell back against Kiya. 'Help me,' he rasped. 'I want to see.'

They were more than happy. Together they went back up the tunnel, back to Brinu's home and into the open air.

Evening had come and the air was full of fireflies and pollen. The forest had come back to life. Everywhere the trees were alive, their bark still blackened but their branches heavy with leaves and blossoms. The ground was lush with grass and other plants, and above the Skytree was magnificent.

'It's alive!' Kiya screamed. 'It's *alive!*'

Lyell leaned against the tree, stroking the bark. 'They all are,' he said softly. 'The great trees—all of them are in bloom. I felt it. All over Hylah, the forests have come back. All is as it should be.'

The other elves gathered around the tree, embracing it. Tail swooped and soared through the branches, Vender laughing on his back, and Lyell took it all in with a quiet smile.

'You did it!' Vender crowed. 'I knew you could do it!'

Lyell started to speak, but a movement off to his left caught his eye and he looked up sharply. Someone was coming. He was about to put out his spikes, but then the musty stench hit his nose and he relaxed somewhat.

'Kobolds,' he muttered.

There were only a few of them. The first came limping toward him out of the trees, one leg dragging. From the sound of his breathing he was obviously in pain, and most of the others with him were clearly injured as well.

Lyell met their leader at the edge of the clearing. 'Ferlak. You came back.'

Ferlak's yellow eyes were dim, and one of his fangs had broken off. 'Lyell, help. Hurt, need help.'

Lyell took the kobold by the paw and gently led him over to the tree. The others followed. Vender looked uncertain, but Ferlak blinked at the gnome and said, 'Little gnome friend! Vender!'

Vender's face split into a smile. 'Ferlak, it's you!'

Ferlak slumped down against the tree. 'Many kobolds die,' he growled. 'Humans kill us. We not know where to go.'

'It is all right now,' said Lyell. 'You can stay here and we will take care of you.'

Ferlak patted him. 'You good friend, Lyell elf.'

'But not as good a friend as you, Vender,' said Lyell. He smiled at the gnome. 'Where will you go now? I am sure the humans would welcome you in Vaporcitta, and you could help them find a cure for the plague on your people.'

Vender shook her head. 'Vender's not a doctor,' she said. 'Anyway, the other gnomes were never really my people. I reckon your people are the people you choose. I'm choosing you, Lyell. I'm staying in Silverwood. I like it here, and so does Tail.'

'So be it,' said Lyell.

'But Lyell,' said Kiya. 'Silverwood is a place for elves...' She trailed off uncertainly.

Lyell looked up at the flourishing Skytree. 'This is my forest now, is it not?'

'It is.' Ardrathar bowed his head and the others did the same. 'You saved Silverwood, and you saved the great trees,' the other elf intoned. 'You are the one who was sent to us, to save us all and to take Brinu's place... Lord Lyell Skytree.'

'Blackfletch,' he corrected. 'Well, then, if I am the lord of Silverwood, then I decide who may live here, and I say that Vender is welcome. She saved my life, and she saved yours too. She is worthy. And you, Ferlak—you fought for us. Brinu used you and the other kobolds for his own purposes. But that time is over now. There is no more need for senseless killing. Live here with us, in peace. We have forgotten our old ways, but now we will go back to them. We will live in harmony with the trees, as we did once before, and leave the other races to go their way.'

'But my Lord—' one of the others began.

Lyell shook his head. 'I am your lord now,' he said. 'My word is law. No more killing. There was never any purpose to it, as I realised in Vaporcitta. The great trees are alive again, and it was not murder that made that happen, but friendship and sacrifice. If those trees are all one, then so is Hylah, and so are all those who live in it. That is how it was, and that is how it must always be.'

'He's right,' said Vender. 'I never got it why people should pretend to be nice when they aren't. People should just tell the truth. If they did, then everyone could be friends, like me and Lyell.'

'You could be right,' said Lyell. 'But sometimes the truth is hard.'

'Doesn't matter,' said Vender. 'You should tell it anyway. Unless you're protecting someone,' she added.

Lyell put his head on one side. 'Vender,' he said. 'Lavender of Bluedell. I confess I thought you were a fool once. And you are naïve, it is true. But I think what you just said is one of the wisest things I have ever heard. Lies cost me the one I loved, and they have hurt so many. Perhaps, if people told the truth more often, we could indeed be friends. But old hurts are so hard to cast aside.'

'You just have to forgive people, I reckon,' said Vender.

Lyell thought of Agafya, and he remembered his last words to her. He shuddered. 'I do not believe some things can be forgiven.'

'You are right, my Lord Blackfletch,' said Ardrathar. 'Some things cannot be forgiven.'

'But maybe they *should* be,' said Vender. 'It can't be that hard, can it?'

'Some things are impossibly hard,' said Lyell. 'But you always made such things seem easy, Vender. Perhaps even we have things to learn from you.' He leaned back against the tree, looking up at the fresh leaves as they fluttered in the breeze. Everything had changed now, and it would change again, he knew. But now, after so much fear and uncertainty, his path had become clear to him once more. The Skytree was his to protect now, and so were the others. Not just his people, but Ferlak and the other kobolds, and Vender too. But, as Vender had said, there was no difference now. She and Ferlak were his people as well.

Now, they were one.

24

WOOD AND FIRE

Agafya gave birth in Fivrath, in her family's old quarters. They belonged to her now. She and the other dwarves had spent the months of her pregnancy cleaning up the city as best as they could, and they had closed the damaged gates. Yevgeni and Timur stood guard on the walls, ready in case of a kobold attack, but there was nothing. Still, they would leave nothing to chance.

When the birth came, Vitya and Irina stayed to do what they could, though neither was a healer. Still, it was not a difficult birth, and when it was over Agafya rested and stared in wonder at what Lyell had given her—or what she had taken from him.

Twins.

One was a boy, the other a girl, and they were unlike any infants she had ever seen before, their skin too pale for pure dwarves and their ears pointed like their father's. But both felt hot to her, as dwarves should be, even when they were newly born.

In time, the other dwarves came to see for themselves. They looked uncertain, but pleased.

'The first half elvish children in the world,' Timur murmured. 'Such a strange thing.'

Agafya held them close. 'I name them Eva and Alexei Ivano,' she said proudly. 'They are the future of our people.'

'I will teach them to fight,' said Timur.

'And I will teach them to use their magic, whatever it may be,' said Irina.

'I will teach them the ways of the dwarves,' said Yevgeni.

'I will teach them to read and to write,' said Vitya.

Agafya looked at them, and then at her children, but she said nothing. The determination hardened in her and she made a silent vow.

They are not elves. They are dwarves, and I will teach them to be dwarves. And if it is that their father still lives, they will never see him.

She thought uneasily of the trees. The trees they had found suddenly growing in the streets of Fivrath and around its walls, and one tree in particular—the massive black-barked tree with the red leaves, which had sprang up at the base of Karvbac seemingly overnight. It had been there waiting for them when they first came to the city. None of them could explain where it had come from, and yet Agafya remembered. She remembered the old stories of the great tree that had once grown here—the one her ancestors had called the Fireleaf. And when they had scouted back over the blasted lands, they had seen that Silverwood had suddenly begun to flourish again.

It made no sense. Surely this wasn't possible. No magic could do that.

Still, to Agafya it was a sign. The old ways had come to an

end, and now a new time was dawning. And she, and her children, would be a part of it. The future, whatever it may hold,
belonged to them.

ACKNOWLEDGMENTS

Thanks to Michelle, Nathan, and Josh, without whom this book would not be in your hands today.

ABOUT THE AUTHOR

Born in Canberra in 1986, Katie J. Taylor attended Radford College, where she wrote her first novel, *The Land of Bad Fantasy*. She studied for a Bachelor's Degree in Communications at the University of Canberra, and graduated in 2007 before going on to do a Graduate Certificate in Editing in 2008.

She is also the author of the Fallen Moon Trilogy: *The Dark Griffin, Griffin's Flight,* and *Griffin's War,* as well as the Risen Sun Trilogy: *The Shadow's Heir, The Shadowed Throne,* and *The Shadow's Heart,* and the Southern Star Trilogy: *The Last Guard, The Silent Guard,* and *The Cursed Guard.*